PRISONER OF A PROMISE

Prisoner Of A Promise

by

Quenna Tilbury

Dales Large Print Books
Long Preston, North Yorkshire,
BD23 4ND, England.

British Library Cataloguing in Publication Data.

Tilbury, Quenna
    Prisoner of a promise.

    A catalogue record of this book is
    available from the British Library

    ISBN   1-84262-443-1 pbk

First published in Great Britain in 1978 by Robert Hale Limited

Published in Large Print 2006 by arrangement with
S Walker Literary Agency

Dales Large Print is an imprint of Library Magna Books Ltd.

Printed and bound in Great Britain by
T.J. (International) Ltd., Cornwall, PL28 8RW

ONE

Dr Adam Elliott looked in the plain glass partition at the special patient as he passed down the corridor, but his thoughts were on the nurse standing by the bed.

Nurse Belinda Fenn seemed totally absorbed in the patient; the only one in the silent, three-bed ward. It must be lonely, she thought. Not that he could see those two empty beds. His eyes were still bandaged after his operation. Yet, she thought, closing her own soft brown eyes experimentally, one could surely sense the loneliness?

Sensing things was just what he did. He sensed that there was someone near him. He said sharply, 'Is it my nurse?' so she took his hand and said, quietly, 'Yes, I'm here.'

'You don't know what those three little words mean to me,' he said with a twisted smile, and he clung on to her hand with a grip that hurt. 'How long have you been by my bed?'

'Just a few minutes,' she said, totally unaware of the tall, strongly built, rugged figure of Adam Elliott, whose keen grey eyes were always searching for her.

'How long will you stay?' the patient

7

pursued. 'I know you go to the other end of the room and sit writing.'

'I'll stay by you for a while,' she said tranquilly. He was being specialled all the time and she was forbidden to let him know. In the ordinary way he could be in the Intensive Care unit, but it was not quiet enough for this particular case, so Spanwell General Hospital – never really up-to-date in many ways – had fallen back on yet another old treatment, and one that the ward sister firmly believed was, in some cases, as good as any. She liked to feel that a responsible nurse was by a patient who would probably try to tear off his bandages if he got too depressed. She liked to feel she could glance in the clear glass of the top of the partition as she went by in the course of her many duties, to 'see for herself'. The Intensive Care Unit was remote – downstairs, just outside the theatre, and a long way away, she considered.

Of course, there were snags in everything, and Sister Newman was the first to admit that some very ill patients could be rather unreasonable. This man, for instance, had insisted on having the same nurse by his side night and day, and nothing could make him see it wasn't possible. And that, she thought grimly, was the only reason she had hit on the idea of putting Nurse Fenn's younger sister to sit by him in the older girl's off duties, for their voices were uncannily alike. Let him think his nurse was there all the time – improbable as it may seem, if it was going to help him. She wasn't happy about the arrangement, though, but with so many people passing by, she supposed there was little that could go wrong, though she herself didn't really consider that Nurse Penelope Fenn was taking her job as seriously as she ought to.

Sister Newman sighed. She remembered that, ward sister though she had been for many years, she had been, at the beginning of her training, a most irresponsible probationer nurse, even for those days, and had often been threatened with instant dismissal.

She looked in now, as she passed A-19. Dr Elliott had moved on down the corridor, which was as well, because he didn't agree with this plan at all. But there was Belinda Fenn, calmly, serenely standing by the patient's bed, speaking to him reassuringly in that low soft voice that was so soothing. Sister Newman thought that if she were ever ill, she would like to be nursed by that girl, who clearly loved her work.

The patient thought so too, and said so. 'Sometimes, though, I feel that you are in a rather gay mood, giddy almost – but then a young woman can't be expected to be serious and unsmiling all the time.'

Belinda started to say indignantly that she was never in a giddy mood, but the words were strangled in her throat. She suddenly remembered her young sister Penny, who was due to relieve her in a very short while. Penny was never anything else but giddy. 'Do you mind the giddy moods?' she murmured.

'I like all your moods,' he admitted. 'And I like you, too. Very much.'

She smiled in a relieved way. That was running true to form. How many male patients hadn't told her how much they liked her, only to forget her the minute they left hospital! And that was as it should be, after all.

'I wouldn't be happy if you didn't like your nurse,' she said.

'There's a smile in your voice at this moment,' he murmured. 'Tell me what you look like. Hair – what colour? Gold?'

Penny's hair was gold, her own a soft light brown. Oh, well, why not, she thought; let him feel he had guessed right. So she said, 'Gold; corn yellow, gold in the sunlight,' and he looked satisfied.

'What colour eyes?' so she felt she should be consistent and say, 'Blue. A really blue blue, not greeny blue.' For her own eyes, light brown and in her own view rather ordinary, wouldn't interest him at all, she was sure.

Then he surprised her by saying, 'And you are twenty-three. What a nice age. And you have been engaged once, but are now completely free?'

10

She was so taken aback that she didn't answer. He seemed to have mixed up her description with Penny's. Her own age and love life but Penny's colouring. Oh, yes, she thought, with a flash of annoyance – that would be Penny again. Penny loved to romanticise, and to imagine herself in different situations. Belinda remembered with wry humour the time that Penny had told old Mrs Hurst that she had only been adopted and was badly treated by the Fenn family, and old Mrs Hurst had been so incensed that when Belinda came to do her back and pressure points, the old lady had insisted on another nurse doing it instead. But that was some time ago, and Penny had been good for how long? Two whole months, it must now be! Two months since she had had that awful interview with her seniors and only Belinda's pleading had enabled her to stay on at the hospital; that and the fact that their father was a local G.P. and their mother had been a nurse.

Belinda sighed, but the patient was waiting for her answer. 'I wonder how you came by that information,' she murmured. It was all over and done with – that old affair with a young houseman called Derek Hollidge. She thought in amazement that she could now say his name to herself, and not get a single reaction, whereas at one time (at Penny's age, that was) the mere thought of his name made Belinda feel all shaky and excited.

The patient was indignant. 'But *you* told me – yesterday. Don't you remember?' Then he was at once contrite. 'It's my fault, insisting on you staying by me all the time. All those hours of watching. Most selfish of me. You must be asleep on your feet. But there it is: I feel that if you leave me, my life-line will go. You won't leave me, will you?'

'No, I won't leave you,' she said. She had been instructed to say that. It was no business of hers to wonder how the patient, who was apparently a sensible, even a clever man, in ordinary life, could be so gullible as to believe that one nurse could stay by him all the time. People might have done that in days gone by, nursing at home in their own family, but he should know that a special nurse in hospital was unusual anyway, and she was changed every so many hours, on a rota, for rest and other duties. But he was the guinea-pig patient of Sir Maxwell and if he came through this, it would be a great feather in the hospital's cap. 'But what else did I tell you yesterday, that I don't seem to remember clearly today?' she asked carefully.

'You asked me how old I was, and if I was married, and if I had more than one car and a town flat as well as an estate in the country. And you were most anxious to know if I approved of Borzois.'

She looked blankly down at him. Borzois?

Was he raving again, as he had been just after the operation, because of the special drugs that had had to be used? Or ... dreadful thought ... had Penny been amusing herself again?

Worse, why had he not realised that a nurse could get his age and whether he was married or single, from the notes at the end of the bed? But they were always removed when Penny took over, in case she unwisely read them aloud to the patient. Belinda knew that Fergus Jopling wasn't married, and that he was forty-six, a comparatively wealthy man but a tragic one, with the start of another illness showing, and she would never have dreamed of asking any patient such personal questions. She couldn't wait to get off duty to find her young sister, to see just what had been happening.

'I must have been tired,' she said. 'Forgive me, for being so impertinent as to ask such questions.'

'Oh, no, my dear, you of all people must know of such things about me, and all the other things I told you, as well. We had quite a heart-to-heart talk yesterday, and it was high time. I kept nothing back, and I didn't intend to, but I regret you didn't tell me much about yourself in exchange. But here we are, almost at the day when these bandages will be taken off, and we shall know if I can see again, and then – ah, then we shall have to make plans, you and I.'

Now Belinda was really alarmed. What could Penny have been up to? She must tell someone, before it was too late. But that would explode the fact that there had been two of them, and he apparently couldn't tell them apart. *Were* their voices so much alike? Or had Penny been at her old trick of making her voice sound extra like Belinda's by phrasing her conversation in the same way?

The patient's hand suddenly lost its grip on hers, and she realised he had fallen asleep. Soon she would have to relinquish this chair to her sister, and now she was desperately afraid of leaving Penny with him.

She could hear the familiar jaunty footsteps coming smartly along the corridor. She softly left the bedside of the sleeping man, and looked out of the plain glass. Penny, gold curls bobbing in a way to almost shake off the absurd little first-year cap pinned precariously on top, was shamelessly flirting with an up patient, clad in dressing-gown and slippers, on his way to the bathroom.

Suddenly Penny ducked her head and skittered along towards where Belinda stood waiting, and the up patient melted into the bathroom and closed the door. They must have heard Sister, who was making speed towards this ward, but at the last moment she was buttonholed by one of the housemen. Penny, safe for the moment, slipped

14

through the door and stood facing Belinda, her blue eyes wide and innocent. 'Am I late?' she whispered.

'No, but what have you been saying to him?' Belinda hissed back, meaning her patient who was now moving restlessly.

Wilfully Penny misunderstood. 'Well, if a girl can't cheer up any patient who passes her on the way to the bathroom and says it's a nice day, I don't know what the world's coming to!' and her voice disturbed the patient.

No chance now to ask questions, Belinda fumed. 'Don't ask him personal questions,' was all she could manage to whisper, before he awoke and called.

Belinda left her sister to go to him, and slipped quietly out, taking his notes with her. Sister Newman stopped her. 'How is the patient, Nurse?'

Belinda hesitated. Now was the moment to speak, but there were so many things involved here. She couldn't be certain (until she had had time – lots of it – to carefully and insistently question her young sister) whether Penny had really told him an outrageous story about Belinda herself, or whether he had imagined it, lying there. And after all, if he were kept amused and happy, did it matter very much what erroneous impression he got of an old love affair of Belinda's which didn't trouble her any longer? So she said, 'His voice is sounding stronger every day, Sister, and he takes an interest in what is said to him.'

'But he has expressed no alarm over the fact that he is constantly watched by (apparently) one nurse?' and this seemed to be the point that was worrying the ward sister.

'He doesn't express alarm about anything,' Belinda could say with complete truth. And so the moment for voicing her fears, nebulous as they were, passed, and leaving the notes with Sister Newman, Belinda went off duty, to get what rest she could before taking over in the arduous watch of the night hours.

At night, it was cold. A strange dark world of moving shadows, the spot of a pencil torch here and there as nurses went from bed to bed at stated intervals to check the patients were needing nothing. A world in which excitement and hurry could flare up suddenly with an emergency, or stay sterile and almost motionless until the grey unfriendly dawn broke, and those patients who were well enough were dragged from the warm nest of sleep to partake of a cup of tea, and begin the rounds of the day.

Some hospitals had become modernised and didn't disturb their patients so early, but Spanwell General clung to the past where it could, on the grounds that some old habits were not necessarily bad because they *were* old.

Belinda had run out of tooth paste and

hand cream, and decided on a hasty trip to the shops in the next street, before flopping into bed and remembering to put a dark scarf over her eyes as well, before drawing her room curtains in an attempt to shut out the day and get some sleep. An unnatural habit she had never cultivated.

Adam Elliott had followed her to the main doors, with the intention of offering her a lift. He guessed she was bent on a trip to the shops. But someone caught him with an urgent request and by the time he was free, she had gone.

She hadn't even seen him. Her mind was bent on the things she had to buy. This wasn't the main shopping centre of Spanwell, but a scattering of small shops on the outskirts of the town. Hospital personnel were glad of these shops when off duty times were short and difficult, but today none of the shops seemed to stock the things Belinda wanted. She stood looking down that street in frustration. There wasn't time to wait for a bus into town and get one back again. Was there another shop who might just stock what she wanted?

Memories rushed to the fore as she stared at the little hairdresser's where she had once excitedly had her hair swept up in an impossible style for that hospital ball five years ago, at which Derek was to attend. His first ball at their hospital, having just come down from the North. Now what had made her remember that, she thought irritably? The hair style had been too old for her. It had done nothing for her but to make her look pinched and anxious. He had looked past her at the redhead just behind her. What had been her name? Now she was recalling past memories, she made the effort and got it: Marcia Peters. Belinda recalled crying into her pillow that night. How one suffered at eighteen, because a handsome young man isn't looking at one's new hair style that had cost too much, but instead had had his interest caught by a redhead who had just brushed her hair carelessly into a natural curling pony-tail tied with a sophisticated dark brown velvet bow to match her dress. That was Marcia: terrific with seemingly little effort. And when she had achieved what someone else wanted, she had abandoned it.

Belinda – half annoyed with herself, half amused – dived across the road and into the shop, to see if their array of cosmetics would include the brand she wanted, but of course, it didn't. They suggested the new chemist's who had just opened round the corner.

Now running out of time, Belinda shot round the corner, slap into a young man emerging from the chemist's door, with films in his hand, and a camera over his shoulder.

Recognition wasn't mutual. It wasn't until he heard Belinda's voice busy apologising, that he remembered her, and even when he apologised in turn, she hardly recognised him. His face was thinner, he wore glasses with heavy dark frame, and there was a touch of grey already in his dark hair. Already? He was not even thirty, she thought confusedly, as she said, with an effort to avoid the little name she had always called him: 'Derek?' and he, apparently making the same effort to remain formal, in the circumstances, said, 'Belinda?' and the name sounded unfamiliar on his tongue. And though he still held her by the arms, to steady her after their collision, she realised there was no spark. No spark left, she thought sadly. All that old unhappiness, and this just confirmed for her that her first love was dead. Well, it was as well.

She said, 'What are you doing here?' then remembering the things she had to buy, she said, 'Just wait a tick – I just must–' and letting her words trail off, she dashed in the little new shop, found the brands she wanted, and was out again, half expecting he hadn't waited. But he had.

'Well, this has saved me going to the Nurses' Home for you. Where shall we go for this talk? You don't look very worried,' as if it were a continuation of a recent conversation.

'Talk?' she echoed, bewildered, so frowning, he said, 'Well, you did admit in your note to being absent-minded, but you can't be that absent-minded, to have fetched me down from Birmingham to see you specially. Now don't look alarmed, it so happened I was coming down anyway, so it fitted in.'

But she was alarmed. 'What note?' she asked blankly.

He studied her closely. 'Here, you need a cup of tea, and so do I,' and ignoring her protests about not having time, he took her arm and began to march her towards the teashop where they had once met so often. 'It isn't there now,' she told him, so they had to make do with a seedy looking converted shop optimistically called The Blue Bird, further down the road. 'It used to be called Bert's Caff. Bert was a patient,' she told the amused Derek. And then neither of them were amused because he got out the note that had summoned him to see her, and while she read it confusedly, she remembered thinking that this wasn't a joke of Penny's as she had at first feared. It couldn't be.

It started: 'DEAR DEREK,' and it was so like her own handwriting that she could only stare helplessly at it, especially as the main part of the note was so definite, so demanding. 'I'M IN AWFUL TROUBLE AND NEED YOUR ADVICE. I KNOW IT'S A LONG TIME NOW BUT A PATIENT RECENTLY TOLD ME WHERE TO FIND YOU. I HOPE YOU WON'T THINK IT'S A CHEEK ON MY PART BUT YOU WERE ALWAYS SO GOOD WITH ADVICE.' And she was shattered further by

20

the note being signed: 'LULIE'. His little name for her, all those years ago.

'Well?' he asked her, bothered by her shocked white face.

'I didn't send that. I've never seen it before!' she said, but even as she said it, a thought was hammering in her brain. How had the writer known that Derek used to called her 'Lulie'? That silly, private little name.

He put it to her, and she said, almost without thinking, 'But that's odd, because the person who sent this note didn't know what I used to call you. Never Derek, remember?'

'No, that's true, but then you might have gone formal on me since we split up,' he pointed out, and she refrained from saying that in that case she wouldn't have signed herself Lulie. 'And it does look like your writing,' Derek added.

'How would you know?' she flashed. 'I never wrote you any notes.'

'No, but I saw your writing in those notes you had to write up for lectures,' he reminded her. 'Lulie, what's wrong? Why did you want me again?'

She shook her head, wondering how she could convince him that this wasn't from her. 'My dear, I'm so sorry – so very sorry – that somehow you've been brought here for nothing. I didn't send that note, truly I didn't. I wouldn't have. You know me better than that. It was over between us. I didn't even know where you were. Nobody has mentioned you since you went away.' Except the blind patient, her thoughts clamoured, and even he hadn't mentioned Derek by name. But had he known it? Had Penny meddled and given Derek's name? But why? And this note – who had copied her hand-writing so faithfully? Not Penny, surely? And again, why would she, if she had? For mischief? Oh, no, never that, surely.

'I'm so sorry,' Belinda said again, fastidi-ously avoiding the old petname for him, yet unable to be quite formal. She put down her tea-cup with a final gesture. 'I must go back now. I have to sleep for night duty.' But her innate kindness made her hesitate. 'What will you do, having come here on a fool's errand? Have you somewhere to stay?'

He shrugged. 'I can find somewhere. The thing is, I was coming this way anyway. But you, Lulie – are you in trouble? Do you need help? Never mind what's happened between us. Let's scrub the past, and if there's some-thing I can do, now I'm here, you've only to say so.'

Well, she had a worry. She was up to the ears in worry. But it was so nebulous a thing, and she didn't want to tell Derek about it. She couldn't have said why. She shook her head, and said instead, 'What happened to Marcia?'

22

Marcia, who had captivated him that first night of the Ball, but who, for some reason, hadn't managed to hold him. He had turned to Belinda herself after that, but Belinda had been so much in love with him, and it showed. Marcia had played it clever and got him back, leaving the scar of a furious quarrel between Derek and Belinda.

He must have been remembering all that. 'I wish it hadn't happened, Lulie. Why did it have to? You've matured. If you'd been like this then...'

'How's "like this"? Grown up, for instance? Unlikely to go silly over the first young houseman to look at me that way?'

'Maybe. Something else too. Kindness glowing all over you. And you look steady as a rock and, now I come to think of it, quite capable of settling your own difficulties, without writing this scrubby note yelling for help.' He screwed it up and was about to throw it away but she stopped him.

'Let me have it. I must find out who did it. Well, of course it matters. Some pen-happy kid, perhaps, who might go on writing notes as from me, which wouldn't fizzle out like this, but might land me in real trouble.'

Penny? She prayed it wasn't. Derek hadn't even known Penny, though she might have mentioned Penny to him herself. And certainly Penny had told the patient about Belinda being engaged once. She frowned.

'Where's the envelope it came in?'

He said he'd thrown it into the waste bin in his digs. He seemed to be thinking about something else, so she said, 'Well, was it post-marked from Spanwell?' but he hadn't noticed.

'You've got troubles, yourself?' she said, thinking. 'Why did you come to Spanwell?'

'I didn't say I had. I was passing through, on my way to Cheppingstock,' he said, and he looked unhappy all of a sudden, which prompted her to say, 'You never did say what happened to Marcia.'

'We got engaged,' he said unwillingly, and shrugged. 'She passed me up for some big shot in Harley Street, then she came back, and she looked ill. We were to be married. (Well, she wanted it, and I had nothing else lined up, and she was so done up, poor kid.) And then ... well, she disappeared.'

'Disappeared? You mean, the sort of official disappearance that gets into the press, or just ... walking out of your life again?'

'Could be either,' he said, frowning, 'though I keep thinking of the way she looked when she was supposed to be telling me why she had left me before. All sort of cagey, wanting to tell me, but afraid to. You know?'

Well, that was Marcia. Probably keeping her options open, Belinda thought, using an expression the First Years managed to put into every other sentence, just now. 'What

24

are you doing, jobwise?' she pursued. Something was wrong that he still hadn't told her.

'Since I left Spanwell, you mean? Oh, well, I had an offer at a big teaching hospital, then my father got ill and decided he wanted my brother and me to take over the practice, which we did. He retired, but my brother got married and a family was coming along. There wasn't going to be enough for us both, so I got out. Private practice isn't for me. The local G.P. is a dying animal, to my way of thinking.'

'Well, thanks,' she said dryly. 'My father is one, and he seems to be as busy and happy as always, and I don't think my parents are starving.'

'Here and there it's all right, I suppose,' he said. 'But not for me. As a matter of fact, well, I've got another hospital appointment.'

She was still thinking of the note, and didn't appreciate the way he was looking at her, so she said, 'Oh, where?'

'Don't they tell you anything at Spanwell? It's not my favourite hospital but I had to take something.'

Her head came up sharply. There was only one opening that Derek could reasonably apply for just then. 'The new Casualty Officer!' she said in surprise. 'Well, why didn't you say so at first? So that's why you came here. All this stuff about helping me solve my problems and breaking your journey to somewhere else.'

'But it's true, Lulie,' he said earnestly. 'I'm not due to take up my appointment for a day or so, and meantime I'm to meet a chap in Cheppingstock who has some information, so he said on the telephone. I have to meet him tonight. It's about Marcia.'

Penny denied having told the patient anything. That was predictable, Belinda supposed. Sometimes she did lie her way out of trouble. 'But what did you say about me being engaged some years ago? How could you know about that?' Belinda insisted.

Penny's eyes widened in innocence. 'Oh, doesn't everyone know about it? Jill Metcalfe said everyone did, on account of her cousin being here at the time. Her cousin's old – well, your age, that is. She said her cousin knew you and someone called Marcia.'

'Now you look here!' Belinda said severely. 'I don't know what this is all about, but it's over, and there never was anyone called Metcalfe in my set and–'

'No, you've got it wrong, Bel. It's *Jill's* name, Metcalfe. Her cousin was called Tess Upcroft.' Penny was so obliging with information now, that Belinda could have cheerfully shaken her. And of course, that name rang a bell. Tess Upcroft, the gossip of Belinda's set. Nobody liked her. If this Jill was another pest like Tess Upcroft, no wonder old gossip was being dug up.

'Well, whatever her name is, something funny's going on. The patient knew about it and you must have told him.'

'Well, Sister said he'd got to be kept amused, and he wanted to know (he did truly, Bel!) whether you were engaged or if you had ever been. I didn't know it was such a dead secret. Well, I know we don't talk about things at home but that's because Mummy and Daddy are so deadly deep in medicine they never discuss people or interesting things like broken engagements.'

But as always, there was no chance to ask Penny about anything else, such as that worrying note to Derek, and Belinda was not sure that she wanted to discuss that with her scatty young sister. There was enough nonsense, without feeding her information she probably didn't know.

Penny was just going off duty, and Belinda, who had little sleep after all, was faintly envious of all those young ones leaving the wards to go their separate ways until bed-time. Penny would almost certainly be whooping into town with members of her set, who usually had the benefit of transport of boy-friends who, if they didn't own their own cars, could borrow one from home. Will Byford, the chemist's son, borrowed his father's elderly saloon, and Unwin Calder, whose father was the local photographer, very often borrowed one of the three family cars, regardless of whether his father and brothers were willing to lend. Belinda had been anxious about these two boys before, where her sister was concerned, but she supposed it was better for Penny to be out with a crowd of her own friends and two local boys, than a man that Belinda didn't know.

She went on duty, shivering a little. The wards were as warm as ever, but there was a chill inside her. Derek turning up like that, on a request in a note from someone who knew private things about Belinda, such as the name Derek had called her. And the fact that Marcia was missing and Derek worried about her and was going to see a man about her tonight? What man? How had Derek heard about this man? He hadn't said, and Belinda had run out of time and had had to go. And his odd way of telling her about his new post at the hospital, in Casualty. That had been quite puzzling and in a way upsetting.

The patient was sleeping when she went quietly into his room. In this three-bed ward so high above the street, the traffic of the town was muted. Belinda stared down into the now almost deserted street that ran past the hospital and tried to imagine Marcia as Derek had said she looked: almost haggard, her fresh young beauty impaired by ... what? Illness, late nights, or just plain anxiety?

28

Had she continued her nursing training, or gone into some other field?

Marcia had not been like the other girls that Belinda had trained with. It was not easy to decide what she had been like, but it had often shot into Belinda's mind that Marcia was not working on any special commitment. There were girls who were mad about nursing – the practical side – and the girls who liked the written work best. Some were 'born' nurses and others as ham-fisted as could be, but determined not to let the job defeat them. Some had wanted the job because it was somewhere to live in, and with others of their own age group, girls with no home background, girls from abroad. Always there was an acceptable reason for them to be there. But Marcia appeared to have no such reason.

Marcia always gave Belinda the impression that she was just marking time; not doing the job too badly, because she was too proud to be known as a fool at her work, but certainly just doing it until the other thing turned up. But what other thing? Sometimes Belinda could see Marcia as a model, sometimes as an actress. But always there was that artificial quality about her. Even when she was playing up to Derek, to take him away from Belinda, Belinda had felt that it was no real passion or desire to be engaged to him. There was no warmth in

Marcia, that was it, Belinda thought, as she idly watched a man get out of a car and uneasily look up both ways of the quiet street.

Marcia wasn't capable of showing warmth because there was no warmth in her. Belinda remembered the time when they had been on the children's ward together and Marcia had had to do things for a child in great distress, crying for her mother who had been killed in the same accident, but the child didn't know and they had orders not to tell her. Belinda had been so upset herself that she could hardly speak, but not Marcia. Coolly she had ministered to the child and when it had said, 'When is my Mummy coming for me?' Marcia had casually told her, 'Day after tomorrow, duckie.' Belinda had said to her in the ward kitchen, 'Why tell that stupid lie?' but Marcia had merely shrugged. 'Why not?' she had said. 'I have to get her quiet. I don't want the whole ward bawling. By the time she finds out the truth, I shan't be here.'

Marcia wasn't there. She had been transferred to the Male Accident Wing because of an emergency, and the following week she had left the hospital. Belinda had been there when the child had found out the truth. It was not a thing she liked to look back on. She wondered how Derek would fare, married to a girl like Marcia.

The man in the street was behaving oddly.

Standing well beyond the circle of light from the street lamp, he stared hard up at the window, almost as if he knew Belinda was looking down at him, and then he put up his arm in a kind of signal. Then, as two people walked towards him, he vanished into the car, but after they had gone, he cautiously got out again, looking both ways, then quickly crossed the road to the door into the hospital. Just as Belinda was about to open the window a little to lean out and look, the patient moved, restlessly, and tried to turn his head as if he sensed what she was doing.

She glanced quickly over at him and abandoned her interest in the man in the street to go over to the bed and take the patient's pulse.

'Never far away from me, are you?' Fergus Jopling said tiredly. 'What have you been doing today? You escape to your meals when I'm sleeping, I know.'

'How do you know that?' Had Penny broken her word and let him know there were two of them?

'Funny girl, you never remember half the things you tell me!' he chuckled, and then his smile died and he asked, half anxiously, 'Or is it that I imagine them? Tell me that isn't the case!' and now he sounded really upset.

'Well, I don't always remember everything I say,' she temporarised. 'It doesn't matter, anyway, does it? The bandages are coming off in such a little while and–'

'But you must assure me,' he said feverishly. 'Everything you have said – the serious things, I mean – they were true, you did mean them, didn't you? Say they were! Say you meant every word!' and his forehead beaded with sweat.

'Oh, the serious things, of course,' Belinda said hastily, noticing the sharp rise in his pulse beat, and his hectic colour. 'Now don't get into such a fuss, or I'll have to make a rule not to talk to you at all, and that won't be much fun, will it?'

Meaningless small talk, delivered in her soft, reassuring voice; it ought to have settled him. It had before. But this time it didn't. He insisted, 'What we were talking about yesterday – you did mean that, didn't you?'

Now she was in a real quandary. Knowing Penny's form, she had wondered why Sister Newman had let her young sister near this patient. But there had been nobody else who would do, because of the similar voices, and Penny was only supposed to sit by him, call someone if he needed anything.

But something had been said which was worrying him, so Belinda pulled out the stool, sat down near him, and holding his hand in her two warm ones, she said, 'Now look, what's worrying you? You know you must keep calm. Everything's at stake. We have the unveiling to look forward to,' she said, urging a smile at her joke. But he wouldn't respond, so she went on, 'All right, what is it that you think I may not have meant, in all the things we talked about yesterday. Tell me!'

He hesitated, then he said, 'Get out the photograph again. In my locker. When you put it back you said you'd hidden it under the writing case. Why did you do that?'

What had Penny done? With her heart racing, Belinda went to his locker and turned over the things. One thing Penny should have done and hadn't, was to tidy the locker. Things fell out pell-mell, as Belinda opened the door wide.

Grimly she said, 'I'll have to put these things in more securely for a start,' and began to deftly stack things neatly.

'No, don't stop to do that now. The portrait – of my nephew,' he said, in a bothered way.

There was only one portrait, in a folding leather case. An expensive job. Belinda opened it and caught her breath. It was of the most good-looking young man she had ever seen. Penny would be fascinated. She adored good-looking young men. 'All right, I've got it out,' Belinda said. 'What now?'

'Tell me again what you think of it,' he said, so Belinda, one eye on his distressed face, said the one thing she imagined Penny would say. 'What a super-duper fellow!'

The patient's face was a study. Obviously she hadn't said the right thing.

'Well, what did you expect me to say? Perhaps you have a more dignified way of expressing your opinion of your nephew. How about you saying what you think of him?'

'My nephew,' he said slowly, 'isn't every woman's idea of the man in her life, but if a man doesn't look or act in a way to captivate, it doesn't mean that he may not be captivating inside, when one gets to know him.'

'Well, I agree with that,' Belinda said, puzzled. This man in the portrait was extremely captivating, and in case she had picked up the wrong portrait she looked quickly for another, but there was no other. Besides, it said clearly, 'For my Uncle, who has such high hopes of me!' So that rather clinched things.

But the patient wasn't satisfied, and what he said in reply to that, and the name he used, shocked her so much that she even forget about the queer behaviour of the man in the car outside, which was a pity, for by the time she remembered to go and look again, man and car were gone.

And the patient said clearly, 'That wasn't at all what you said about my nephew yesterday ... *Lulie*.'

TWO

Dr Elliott had no need to come over to the hospital, but he knew that Belinda was on this special duty and he was worried. He had seen her young sister in action too often, and now Belinda had a crease in that smooth forehead of hers, that hadn't been there before.

She was about to be relieved for her meal. The patient was sleeping soundly, induced sleep to relax him for the uncovering of his eyes the next day. There was a great deal of anxiety about it.

As Belinda went down the corridor, relieved by one of the night staff, Adam Elliott caught her up. 'Just going down to eat, Nurse?' he asked.

She looked up at him with a smile. There was a lot of her father in Adam Elliott, she had often thought. Here was a man who could be a rock for a girl to lean on. But, rumour had it, he wasn't free. He was often seen squiring Hope Kingston, Sir Maxwell's pretty niece. It was said to be a family friendship, but it made sense. Dr Elliott was steadily going up the ladder of success, and to marry the niece of the ophthalmic surgeon was surely good sense, especially if he liked her all that much, as he seemed to. With flawless complexion and a flair for clothes and hair styles, Hope Kingston was surely all that an up-and-coming doctor could desire.

She nodded, and said, 'Although heaven knows, I never do feel like food at this unlikely hour. Some nurses can eat heartily, though.'

'Your young sister, for instance? She was starving, I heard her say, not so long ago, and it was as cold and unfriendly a night imaginable.'

They both smiled, sharing amusement over the vivacious Penny. But Adam had something to say and very little time in which to say it. 'What's worrying you, Nurse, about Fergus Jopling?'

There was the creasing of her forehead again. He wanted to smooth it out. She hadn't Penny's provocative prettiness, but a deeper quality; perhaps a serenity in that face, which had nothing to do with mere good looks. She said slowly, 'It's ... it's nothing I ought to worry about. I'm sure Sister knows best and I ought to leave it to her to worry about.'

'Try worrying me with it,' he suggested.

'I'd like to,' Belinda confessed, 'but it's so involved, I don't honestly know where to start.'

'Something in his manner? Is he worried?'

She walked soberly by Dr Elliott and as always before, she felt how strong he was. How dependable. His craggy face could crease up into a warm smile just when one seemed to need it. He was so big, so capable, so utterly ... right, she thought in surprise. But she had no reason to burden him with her troubles.

So, fighting down the urge to confide in him, she said diffidently, 'It's this ... secret doubling up of my sister and myself.'

'What about it? Trouble?' he frowned.

'No, not exactly, but I can't be convinced that such an intelligent man doesn't know there are more than one of us. It isn't in reason.'

'When one has come through what he has, and been under sedation, and a great deal of pain,' he reminded her, 'time has little reality. Neither has anything else, I imagine, except the voice one trusts, the person one thinks is always there.' He glanced quickly at her, remembering something. 'That young sister of yours, has she expressed any thought on this?'

Belinda was convinced she ought to tell him what was bothering her, but it might get Penny into trouble, and after all, she had no proof. So she said, 'It's just the discrepancy in what he says, that is a bit bewildering. Of course, we're both bound to talk to him of different things—'

'Oh, I see, yes, and you can't ask him what was said to him the last time without betraying that there are two of you, and ruining this very successful plan of Sister's,' he said quickly.

Belinda flashed a grateful smile at him. 'That's exactly it,' she said. 'If only I knew what had been said to him when my sister was with him!'

It was a comical smile he directed down at her. 'Ever thought of asking your sister?' he murmured.

She looked severely at him. 'I can see, Dr Elliott, that you have neither a young sister nor a young brother. They don't always react to the older brother or sister as they should.'

'Don't I know it!' he retorted, pulling a wry face. 'I have a young cousin who was brought up as a young brother. Of course, I always thought that as he wasn't really my brother, that made him feel rebellious when I treated him as one. But no, I do see your point. No joy there, is there?'

She nodded. It was getting her nowhere, either.

But suddenly Dr Elliott said, 'Look here, I can see you're worried, and it might be something I could clear up. I gather if you knew the answers to some of the things the patient expected you to, all would be well, eh? Well, why don't I drop in for a chat with the patient and do some careful detective work? Would that help?'

She turned to him, her face radiant. 'Oh, it would, it would! I've been so worried, really. It's ... oh, it's the odd things he comes out with, that really my sister couldn't be expected to know.' She frowned. Sooner or later she would have to disclose that Derek Hollidge, the new Casualty Officer, was once engaged to her. She drew a deep breath to tell him now. Why not? Sooner rather than later. But a nurse shot out of Women's Medical and said, 'Oh, there you are, Dr Elliott! Could you come...' and the moment was lost.

That was always the way, in hospital. Never a chance for an uninterrupted discussion, and this was a very nebulous subject, anyway. She went down to her meal, and wondered if any good would come out of Dr Elliott's idea, after all. Would the patient talk about things he considered to be private? Belinda realised that although she had been with this man for some time, specialling him, she didn't really know him as a person. It was Penny who had apparently got into deep conversation with him. Penny who was so garrulous that at times it was worrying.

It was mutton stew, and Belinda had to force herself to eat some of it, but it was a struggle. She had always been like this on night duty. She would have loved a cup of tea and some thin bread and butter. That would really have refreshed her. But one had no choice at Spanwell General.

She was called to the telephone as she left the dining-room. It was her father. 'I wondered if I might catch you, Bel, just as you came out of supper. Was I right? You've eaten? And I knew it was your turn on nights.'

'Yes, and do you know what time it is, Daddy? How come you are up so late?'

'You must be joking,' he said, trying to laugh. 'I'm talking quietly, because your mother's asleep upstairs, but the fact is, I've only just come in. Mrs Turner's had another miscarriage, poor woman, and frankly, I'm not tired. Well, not sleepy, that is. Got things on my mind. You, for instance.'

'Me!' Belinda asked, puzzled. She hadn't got long to stay here talking, and her father of all people must surely know that. 'What is it, Daddy? There's nothing wrong with me – nothing that won't be put right when I come off nights.'

'Well, it's this patient you're specialling,' her father said diffidently.

'How would you know about him?' Belinda asked slowly.

'Penny rang. She seemed a bit worried.'

'Penny ... worried?' Belinda sounded sceptical.

Her father said, 'Yes, well, it did sound a

bit odd at the time, for Penny to worry about anything, let alone what you were getting up to, but she's been at her mother. She wants to leave nursing, too, and I think she switched to you when her mother got a bit fed-up with the thought of Penny chucking nursing and going into hairdressing.'

'Hairdressing! But I haven't heard anything about this. When did Penny telephone Mummy?'

'Don't get upset, Bel. It's a temptation, I suppose, because we don't live many miles from the hospital, but Bel, if it's the real thing with this patient, perhaps I'd better come over and have a chat with you about it. It's all rather worrying.'

She made a small exasperated noise. Time was not on her side and he had never been one to listen patiently to explanations. 'Daddy, listen! I can't stop now, but I can put your mind at rest. There is no reason for you to come here. No reason for either of you to worry. But I'll have a go at Penny and see what she's up to, because she's causing me worry, if you want to know. I suppose she's just playing up to change her career, which is no new thing. But believe me, there's no question of any "real thing" business where I'm concerned, and certainly nothing at all between me and the patient. Whatever next! Really, just wait till I see Penny.'

'Now, Bel, don't upset her, or she'll just

41

leave and come straight home,' he fretted. 'You know what she's like!'

'All right,' Belinda said quickly. Her father sounded agitated, and he really did work himself into the ground. He was the sort of old-fashioned G.P. who liked to feel needed, who never minded being called out in the middle of the night, but who flayed himself when he lost a patient, or an unsuccessful confinement, as tonight. 'I tell you what. I won't speak to Penny. I'll wait till my next day off and then I'll come home and talk to you – to you and Mummy. How's that? And don't worry about Penny or me until I've seen you. I must dash now. 'Bye. Don't work too hard!' and with that vain hope, she put down the receiver and ran.

But her next day off didn't see Belinda at her home. Too many things happened before the next week was out. And the most disquieting thing that happened was concerned with the patient, Fergus Jopling.

In the small hours, when the cold intensified, and the resistance is at its lowest ebb, the patient woke. Belinda was at his side in an instant. He groped for her hand and he said, 'Speak to me. Let me hear your voice. I have the feeling that one day I shall wake up and it won't be your voice and that everything will fall to pieces around me and I shan't want to live!'

42

He didn't usually dramatise. He had a quiet voice, a precise way of putting words together. She couldn't imagine him using slang or following any of the popular fashions and fads. His sudden pronouncements was all the more surprising. 'And don't go to the door to call the ward sister, excellent woman though she may be,' he continued. 'Only you can deal with this, Lulie.'

'Very well,' she said after a moment. 'But please – don't call me "Lulie". It's rather a ... well, just one person gave it to me and I'd rather you didn't use it.'

He looked surprised, pained. 'But yesterday you were so cordial and begged me to call you that. You also said that you had quite got over that old affair and to prove it, I was to call you your little name, that everyone used.'

'But that's "Bel",' she corrected him, gently. 'You must have been just going off to sleep and got muddled. Never mind, what was it you wanted to say?'

'What we've decided to do, you and I – are you happy about it?' he pressed, to her utter dismay. What, for heaven's sake, was it he thought they'd decided?

'Tell me why you think I shouldn't be, if I was happy about it before,' she temporarised.

'Well, you did say you'd got over that old affair and were ready to take up the threads again,' he said slowly, probingly.

43

Great heavens, he didn't think he was persuading her to marry him, did he, she thought, in agony? A chill thought entered her mind that Penny must really be responsible for this, because Penny had hinted to her father that Belinda was about to become engaged to the patient.

'I must have been trying to be brave yesterday,' Belinda said, and made up her mind that as soon as this man's bandages came off the next day, she would ask for a transfer. And never again would she put herself in this position so that young Penny, spoiled baby of the family, the darling of her parents, could do this to her! It just wasn't fair. It was all a game to Penny.

'You mean you haven't got over that old affair?' Mr Jopling pressed.

'Mr Jopling,' she said firmly, 'I know you have been talked to about a number of things, but only to keep you amused and interested. It isn't really allowed, you know, and it would be frowned on if it were to get to Sister's ears. I have tried to take your mind off your troubles, to make the hours go by more quickly when you are awake, but to be honest there's only one thing I want in the world.'

'I know what it is,' he smiled, much to her surprise. 'It's understandable that you want a lot of money. Who doesn't? Money for pretty clothes and cars and travel and servants. Well, you'll have all that, I can assure you, for your golden voice has kept me interested, and that is worth all the money in the world.'

'But Mr Jopling–' she tried to break in to deny indignantly, but he was determined to finish what he had to say.

'Sometimes you are just kind and firm, as you are now. But at other times you are gay and entertaining and say outrageous things to me and tell me ridiculous stories that I don't always believe, but I'm quite sure you wouldn't have led me to think you had lived such an adventurous life if it weren't true.'

'Mr Jopling–' she tried again.

'Those gay moods have been my lifeline, and I don't know what I would have done without them, so I can forgive the moods in between, like now, when you are obviously not gay or outrageous. You're cold,' he said suddenly, holding her hand. 'What time is it?'

It wasn't just her hands that were cold. She had been growing cold all over, and more disturbed every minute, during that speech of his. Her mind was torn between the two aspects: what had he promised Penny and what had Penny told him? But more important, as he had already distinguished between the two completely different moods of his nurse, how was it he couldn't divine that it was, in fact, two different people?

Belinda gulped, certain that she must find

out, and now. Tomorrow might be too late. 'It's three in the morning, and we all get cold hands at that time. Never mind, I may not be gay just now, but if I can't keep you amused, you shall entertain me. By telling me which story you enjoyed most from me.'

He appreciated that. He chuckled, in a spent way. 'That's easy: the one about that properly developer who believed you when you said you were going to buy the block with the hairdressers' in it. So you shall when you get my money!'

She sat back limply, and felt frankly horrified. Hairdressers! Yes, that would be Penny's great interest! But did she have to lie about knowing a property developer and making him such a bogus offer? 'And you *liked* that story?' she weakly asked the patient.

'Yes, but I must admit I like to hear you tell me about the lectures in which you stand out so well. I can believe that. You are a born nurse! I know it! And that is the thing I prize so much.'

Lectures? Penny standing out well in them? Penny didn't attend half the lectures she should, and usually her work was so bad that she was constantly being threatened with dismissal. Her best friend sometimes helped her with the notes but her lecture material was never up to scratch! No, Penny had adroitly mixed both girls up, in this way, because she must have realised that any nursing that had been done for him, had been done by Belinda herself, and Belinda, as everyone knew, was very very good at her job.

'You won't have to worry about nursing after tomorrow, I'm sure,' she said, with more firmness than she felt. For herself, tomorrow couldn't come soon enough.

'Oh, but even after tomorrow you and I will be very close,' he urged. 'Closer, a great deal closer, in fact,' and his voice sounded so satisfied that she was conscious of a deep-seated fear. She had better not wait for Dr Elliott to talk to this man. She must question Penny herself, even under the threat of taking her to Matron's office, for this time Penny's mischief had really gone over to the danger limit.

Then the patient started talking about where his wealth lay. 'Perhaps you didn't know that I have interests in chemical research laboratories and copper mines? I also happen to own a chemical firm – you know, the sort that makes pills, patent medicines and things.' He was talking to her in the tone one often applied to Penny, just to make sure she understood.

'That must be very nice for you,' Belinda said firmly. 'But I have never wanted big money. I'm a contented person. I love my work–'

'I know, I know, but there are times when you long for a yacht, and a car that turns

47

people's heads – you've told me so and I quite understand. And you will get those things.'

There was the tiniest thread of sound at the door. She turned her head sharply to look. Dr Elliott stood there. He must have heard that. She half rose but he shook his head and signalled her to stay where she was. He also pointed to the ward kitchen, and went quietly away. He liked a cup of cocoa about this time. Her best friend, Zoë Allen, would make it for him. Zoë was infallibly cheerful, night duty or days, and she would cheer him up.

But before five minutes had passed, the patient – tired out with so much talking – had dropped off again. Zoë looked in, and made a sign of drinking and pointed to the kitchen, prepared to sit herself in Belinda's seat until she came back.

It was unlikely that the patient would wake again just yet. His sleeping pattern was fairly regular after so much sedation.

Belinda softly went out, believing Zoë had left a cup of cocoa in the ward kitchen for her. She had, but she had also left Dr Elliott drinking his. He got up and stood watching her. 'Come in, and drink this. It's good,' he said.

'Did you hear what the patient was saying?' she asked without preamble.

'I did. You'd got him fairly happily tiring

himself out, I see,' he remarked with satisfaction.

'You don't understand, Dr Elliott, he seems to think he's arranged to give me a lot of money. It must have been my young sister!'

His smile slipped for a moment, then he grinned broadly. 'Well, don't worry. He'll change his tune tomorrow. If it's success, when the bandages come off, he'll forget everything he's promised. And if it isn't a success...' His mouth turned down. 'He won't be in much of a mood to distribute largesse that way either, I imagine.'

She could never make anyone see what a pest Penny was. Dr Elliott couldn't see any wrong in what her sister had been up to. Some of the weariness that was flooding through her, made her shoulders sag. She silently drank her cocoa and thought of her father, who was also thinking kindly of Penny, but who was wondering worriedly what Belinda herself had been up to. But of course, her parents had always been protective about Penny. It was, Belinda thought, perhaps because Penny had such a baby face. Such an endearing face.

Dr Elliott said, 'I expect you'll be in for a few days' leave if all goes well tomorrow, Nurse?' and she said she hoped so. 'What will you do with it, that precious batch of a few days off?' he smiled.

'Sleep, I expect, if I can,' she admitted, with

a slow smile that he couldn't drag his eyes from. 'Do you expect Sir Maxwell's work will be successful, tomorrow, I mean?' she felt forced to ask him. If only she could look forward into the future and see what would happen!

'We all expect success tomorrow,' Dr Elliott smiled. 'Don't worry.'

'Has he always been successful?' she pursued, without quite knowing why. If only tomorrow would come, so that she could escape.

Dr Elliott hesitated briefly, before saying, 'As an ophthalmic surgeon, I don't remember a single time when he didn't have success, Nurse,' and he put down his cup and walked out, leaving her wondering what there was in Sir Maxwell's career or life that hadn't gone right. Later, looking back, she often wondered how different things might have turned out if only she had known.

THREE

Belinda had called it the unveiling. Well, the ceremony of removing the patient's bandages was akin to that event, in excitement, triumph, crushing despair, whatever the way it went. There seemed to be quite a number of people in the room, Belinda included. It would have been Belinda anyway, and not Penny, because Penny was only a junior. Belinda should have been off duty at that time, but the patient had been rather difficult until he had been assured that his special nurse would be present. He held her hand, as if afraid she would escape before he could see her with his own eyes.

Belinda had tried to speak to Sister personally before this happened. She had passionately not wanted to be there. But there had been an emergency not long before, and nobody had had time to spare for the sort of conversation *that* would have been, Belinda reflected wryly; explosive, to say the least! How could she buttonhole Sister to ask such a question as whether the patient were now to be told that there had been two of them and that between them they had told him different stories? As she thought about it, now they were all assembled, it seem a superficial worry. What would the patient care about what had happened before, once he had got his sight restored?

And of course, if he couldn't see, then everyone would be in a complete flap and it wouldn't matter either, this odd problem of hers. No, she was – as always – bedevilled with what her young sister had been doing, she thought. That was really the underlying worry, and even that would fade, if Fergus

Jopling had his sight restored, for surely he would be allowed to go home?

She had seen this sort of thing happen before. In her second year, she recalled. Her young sister had never seen this and she doubted if Penny would have felt she was missing something. Belinda also recalled that she had promised to speak to her father about Penny, 'when all this was over'.

She dragged herself back from her tortuous thoughts, and noted that the excitement in the room was being played down. Sir Maxwell didn't look too happy, Belinda thought. Sister Newman was frankly anxious. Dr Elliott was there, too, but one couldn't tell what thoughts were chasing each other behind that craggy face, she had learned. He was very good at hiding his thoughts if he wanted to. So, with the curtains pulled against the glare of sudden sunshine, the bandages were at last removed.

Belinda supposed afterwards that she hadn't really expected that the patient would be able to see. There was just a concerted small gasp of satisfaction, such a soft little gasp, from the people concerned, because Fergus Jopling's light grey eyes were focusing. Sir Maxwell bent over him, asking him questions; the others closed in, and Belinda – sensing no more than a queer light-headed feeling – tried to disengage her hand to escape. But the patient held on to it.

Then the surgeon backed away and asked quietly what Fergus Jopling found he could see, and whether it was clear or misty. Fergus Jopling raked the room with his eyes, slowly, carefully. 'I can see all of you, fairly clearly,' he said at last, 'but where is my nurse? My usual nurse?' and he looked rather accusingly at Belinda.

Several voices said, in consternation, that this was his usual nurse. Consternation because he would have to be kept very calm. They all knew why. And clearly he was very agitated indeed. Sister nodded sharply at Belinda, who spoke to him. 'I *am* your usual nurse,' she said. 'But it's all over now. You won't need me, now, will you? And isn't it splendid?'

He was far from pleased. '*You're* my nurse?' She flushed a little at his disappointed tone. 'But my nurse has fair hair and blue eyes. Although it's the same voice.'

The others were looking first at Belinda and then at Sister, and Belinda was waiting for permission to tell him there were two of them, but Sister Newman shook her head fiercely, and this was endorsed by Sir Maxwell. Too many times there had been a relapse and any special arrangement that had been made at first might have to be hastily resorted to again, and it didn't help if the patient discovered what they had been doing. This man would undoubtedly feel cheated.

Belinda said, 'You seemed to think I had fair hair and blue eyes, and you were so ill at the time that it didn't really seem to matter enough to correct your guesswork. Now it didn't really matter, did it?'

'Yes, it did,' he snapped, then he relaxed his tone. 'But it can't be helped. Were the other things true that you told me?'

Thinking he meant her age, her averages at work, she nodded, and said, 'Yes, of course, Mr Jopling.' So for the moment he seemed satisfied. He would have to wear dark glasses for the time being and not have bright sunshine streaming in. He half listened to this, his mind obviously on other things. Belinda gently broke away and went out, leaving Sir Maxwell and the doctors to talk to the patient about future treatment. Now they were quietly pleased, a little puzzled that the patient also wasn't pleased.

Penny came out of the linen room, looking scared. 'How did it go?' she asked Belinda, who was going off duty to get some sleep. Her night duty stint wasn't over yet.

Belinda said, 'Stop worrying. He can see, though he's fed up that he's been thinking of his nurse as having golden hair and blue eyes!' she finished severely.

Penny looked even more unhappy. Then suddenly she started to laugh. 'Oh, the silly man, as if it mattered. He's old, and he kept asking me things.'

She turned as if to go. Somehow that seemed to have satisfied her. But it hadn't satisfied Belinda. 'No, don't escape,' she said sharply, holding on to her young sister. 'That reminds me. You haven't yet told me what else you said to him. What made you talk about me? He knew my special little name!'

'Well, what does it matter that we call you Bel at home?' Penny protested, leaving Belinda wondering whether her sister was wilfully misunderstanding or innocent of having told the patient she was called Lulie by some people. And the thing Belinda wanted to know most of all was who had sent that note to Derek, and why. She said now, 'Did you ever know who ... who I was going around with when I first came here? Now think – I want the truth. I won't be mad at you but I must know!'

Now Penny was getting impatient. 'Oh, does it matter? Actually old busybody Tess Upcroft didn't know. At least, she thought it was Derek Somebody or Desmond Something or other, but she didn't know the name. That reminds me – never mind your old beau. Just take a look at the new Casualty Officer. Now his name is Derek and he's super duper! Honestly! All my set are mad about him. He started today.'

That speech had the ring of truth about it so Belinda accepted that it was no work of her sister's that that note had been sent. But now the mystery deepened, for *who* had sent it to Derek, if it hadn't been young Penny?

And then Sister and the doctors came out of the patient's room and Penny made another bid to escape. But Sister wanted to see her. She asked Belinda to go into her office too, and Dr Elliott and Sir Maxwell went in as well. Penny's eyes widened.

'Don't be frightened, Nurse,' Dr Elliott said kindly. Although he had said Penny was a nuisance, she amused him, Belinda could see.

Penny looked gratefully at him and gulped. Belinda realised she was still holding the back of her sister's dress. Penny was trying to wriggle free so she let go, biting her lip in annoyance. There was no need to play the big sister so heavily, she told herself. Sister was talking in her moderately severe voice.

'This is no reflection on you, Nurse,' she told Belinda, and to Penny, she resumed, 'I think you can perhaps help us, Nurse. The patient is upset because he found that your sister was not of the colouring that he had been led to expect – your colouring. Can you shed any light on that?'

Penny struggled with herself. The struggle was so obvious and rather endearing (wasn't she always like that, Belinda told herself wrathfully) that the men present tried to hide their smiles. Penny said at last, 'Well, I don't want to get my sister into trouble,' and the virtuous tones were so thick that the long-suffering Belinda felt like shaking her, 'but as a matter of fact, when he asked me what my hair was like, I told him, because I had been briefed to tell him what he wanted to know, and the same as the colour of my eyes,' she went on in a rush, 'only then I thought what would happen when my sister came on duty, so I thought when he asked me my age, I'd better say her age, and things about her, only I couldn't unsay the things about me, and it was a ... a bit difficult,' she finished with a comical rush. 'I did try to do what was right and he asks questions at such a rate, and anyway, it didn't seem to matter, me being just a junior and of no count.'

This appealed to everyone except Belinda, who knew how little that last-minute modesty bit amounted to. Sister said, 'Well, that explains it. It was very brave of you, Nurse, to own up. Don't think another thing about it. But keep out of his room in future. You may go.'

Penny didn't go. She looked as if there was a lot more she ought to say. She stood looking very wretched, about to speak, then not speaking. Sister said, 'Is there something else you have to tell us, Nurse?' but that question took away all Penny's new-found bravery and she shook her head fiercely, so Sister sent her away. Belinda was released to go after her, but not quite quickly enough to catch Penny before she had vanished from sight.

What had Penny been about to say, Belinda worried? It nagged at her for hours afterwards.

Adam Elliott got free of that meeting as quickly as he could and he was successful in catching Belinda. 'What was all that about?' he asked quietly, as he walked down with her to the door.

'I don't know,' she said wearily. 'All I do know is that my sister is off the hook, and I'll be in any trouble that comes along.'

'What ... trouble were you anticipating?'

'I can't tell you in just a minute or two like this, though I would like the benefit of your advice,' she said earnestly. 'You see, my father telephoned me as I was leaving my meal last night, and he was so worried, but I had to soothe him down. He's not sleeping much.'

'Worried about ... your young sister? Let's see, he's a G.P., isn't he?'

Belinda nodded. 'And my mother was a nurse. They both so badly wanted us two girls to go into nursing but Penny's worrying them. She... Oh, I suppose I shouldn't say this until Penny says something about it.'

'Don't worry,' he said, with a kind little smile. 'She wants to escape the serious life that nursing is now showing itself to be, isn't that it? Don't look so appalled. You forget it is my unenviable duty to take the Lambs' lectures sometimes, and your young sister is my biggest headache. Don't say "How"? I couldn't tell you.' He thought about it. 'She sits there looking up at me, eyes wide and innocent. Others may be larking or passing notes or going to sleep but not your sister. But I know – and this is what worries me – that behind those eyes, that brain is working on something that has nothing whatever to do with my lecture.'

Belinda looked near tears. 'So you've noticed it too! I wasn't mistaken. I wish I knew what it was, too.'

'You could tell me a lot of things you do know, which might give me a clue,' he reminded her. 'You ought to, too. For your own sake, and your parents' sake. They don't want further worry.'

They had reached the door. 'I'll walk you to the Nurses' Home. What I was thinking was, you'll be off duty the day after tomorrow. How about a meal? I can just cram it in. I could pick you up in my car at the end of this road at six thirty and drive you into Cheppingstock. I know a quiet place with good food and service, and we could unload about what we know of your sister's antics. I keep getting the odd feeling that it's to the patient's advantage, too,' he said quickly, as Belinda seemed about to protest. 'You must have seen how upset he was today, when he looked at you.'

Belinda had a brief struggle with herself. She wanted to talk to him so badly, but knowing what the hospital grapevine was like, she dreaded to be taken out to a meal, even to talk 'shop'. Hope Kingston would find out and there would be a great deal of trouble. Belinda was sure. But it wasn't her suggestion, it was Dr Elliott's, and there was her father to think of. If something could come out of this 'date', then it didn't much matter if it did get all over the hospital, if it could clear up what Penny was up to, and clear it up to the patient's satisfaction. So she said, 'Yes, I'd like that, Dr Elliott. And meantime, I must telephone my father and try to stop him worrying. You didn't ... manage to talk to the patient, did you, as you promised?' she asked, as an afterthought.

'Well, yes, I did,' he said, hesitating. 'He was rather cagey about any mention of his nurse. It struck me he might just have guessed about our arrangement, but when I suggested to Sister Newman just now, that we tell him the truth, she was absolutely adamant. And you nurses are under *her* wing, not mine. I can't claim that such a course would be good for the patient or not. After all, he's chiefly Sir Maxwell's ... at least, he has been, up till now...' and as if feeling he had said too much, Dr Elliott abruptly finished the conversation and left her.

Belinda slept better that day and when she telephoned her father, she felt more braced to tackle the problem they had.

'About Penny, Daddy, that patient we were looking after has got his sight back, no further problems, and Penny won't have to go near him. Now I can tell you that it was a secret arrangement – he thought it was just one nurse because our voices were alike – and the silly little idiot let him think it was only her then she got scared and told him about me, and he's got a mixed impression of us both. Don't worry – he's had his bandages off today and I expect he'll go home soon.'

There was a little silence at the other end, then her father said, 'Bel, you're not hiding anything from me, are you? All this rubbish about the two of you and the patient not being able to tell you apart. That wasn't the problem at all. Penny was worried about you and your marriage – you know the rule about nurses and patients.'

'Yes, you said that last night, and I told you, remember, that I didn't know what you were talking about! Don't let Penny fool you with her wild tales.'

'You always were against Penny!' he said tiredly.

'So you always said, but you know in your heart that isn't true,' Belinda reproved him. 'She irritates me – I'll admit that. She irri-

61

tates a lot of people. But I'm always trying to keep her out of trouble. Do remember that, Daddy.'

'Why did you telephone? You said you'd come home!'

'I thought it would put your mind at rest that Penny's off this special duty. As to the other things, I think she's going through a period of finding the work is hard and she wants to get out. Do be firm and don't let her, Daddy. Hairdressing or anything else needs hard work and application, and you've always said that one shouldn't change horses in midstream or in fact to give up before the job's finished.'

'Yes, but Penny's so young,' he sighed.

'Just the same age of hundreds of other student nurses,' Belinda laughed. 'Daddy, she's the baby, I know, but don't spoil her too much. She must learn to stand on her own feet, and you ought to try and make her see that people won't like her if she does these mischievous things.'

'What mischievous things?' he asked quickly.

Belinda could have kicked herself for saying that. At last she said, 'All the mischievous things she gets up to and has to be baled out. I usually bale her out and I don't tell you because you worry about her.'

'I'm more worried about you, Bel. You had a bad time with that first young man of yours. Sure you're not entangled with a patient?'

Belinda sighed. It was no use, she just must chase Penny up and pin her down to confess what she'd done, even if it meant that her father had betrayed Penny's secret talk with him and her mother. Too much secret business, Belinda thought in annoyance, as she took a step to reassure her father, which she hadn't intended. 'Daddy, as to that, if it will help you to stop worrying, Derek's back. Yes, back here at the hospital, as Casualty Officer. Suddenly. And it looks like our affair is *on* again. Does that satisfy you?'

Her father was silent for a moment. 'Penny didn't tell us that,' he finally said, to which Belinda retorted, 'For once Penny didn't know something personal to me. But she will, and it will be all over the hospital because she can't keep that tiresome little tongue of hers quiet,' the incensed Belinda couldn't help saying.

'Well,' her father muttered, 'I just hope you know what you're doing, my dear, but at least young Hollidge is better than some patient, where there will be nothing but trouble for you. Probably scandal.'

'Oh, Daddy,' Belinda said in despair, but he had rung off.

She went to find Penny. She had no great hopes of running her young sister to earth, but as it happened, Penny was on her way to find Belinda. 'Bel, I have to talk to you,' she said, looking as if she had a load of guilt on her mind.

'All right. Come up to my room,' Belinda said briskly. 'I've just ten minutes before I go on duty. What are you doing over here, by the way?' but Penny had apparently been sent over to change her apron after one of her disasters, and hadn't gone back. 'Bel, I've done something awful. Extra awful.'

'Go on,' Belinda encouraged. 'Get it off your chest and I'll see what I can do.'

'You won't like me after this,' Penny declared.

'Never mind that. I suppose it's what you told Daddy and Mummy, about me going to marry the patient. Is that it?'

Penny's colour drained away. Belinda had never seen her carefree young sister look so horrified. She pushed the girl down into a chair. 'Take it easy! I just haven't much time, so I thought I'd jog your memory, and while we're on the subject, what did you tell them that for? It won't help you to get that hairdresser's career, you know.'

'Hairdresser?' Penny whispered, and then she started to cry, not her noisy crying that she staged in order to get out of a scrape, but scared, miserable crying that was almost silent.

'For heaven's sake, Penny, it isn't that bad,' Belinda said, and gathered her sister into her arms. 'Now do chuck it! This isn't your style. If you've been foolish, for goodness' sake come to the point, so I can go on the wards and while I'm working, I'll have a think what I can do.'

The door opened quietly, and Belinda's best friend, Zoë Allen, looked in, raised her eyebrows at this unusual scene and softly backed out. Penny didn't seem to realise she'd been and gone. She sobbed, 'You'll be wild, I know you will!'

'I expect I will,' Belinda agreed. 'Even more wild if you don't tell me quickly what all this is about. Come on, what did you tell the patient?'

Penny looked up sharply, an odd look passing over her face which Belinda didn't understand. Later she was to think of it, but just then Penny started talking fast, so fast, it was difficult to understand some of the words.

Belinda kept slowing her down, but at last she got some idea of what it was about. When Penny was at last silent, looking doubtfully up at her sister from that tear-streaked young face, Belinda said, with tightened lips, 'As I understand it, the patient told you he was very rich, and had an invalid nephew he wanted to have looked after by a special nurse, a good nurse, for always, and you said you would. A really long-term permanent arrangement. Is that it?'

'Bel, you sound so awful, you're more wild

with me than I expected!' Penny choked. 'I didn't know what to do! He thought I was you, you see. I'd just come on duty and he said I'd done wonderful things to him (meaning you, I expect, because I hadn't done anything except watch him and talk to him and take his pulse and things like that) and he said he wanted such a good nurse for this nephew and he showed me the picture...'

Here Penny broke off again, looking bothered.

'Oh, yes, that picture. What was it you said about it because when he showed it to me, I apparently didn't make the same comment. Come on, out with it!'

'I said he looked a bit ... well, bad-tempered,' Penny gulped.

'You said wha-at? And you were put in there expressly to keep the patient calm and comfortable? Oh, well, never mind. So now you are engaged on your first nursing assignment before you've even qualified, to a very good-looking young man who is a lifelong invalid and you promptly telephone Mummy and Daddy that you want to chuck nursing because you've got cold feet. Am I right?'

'Not quite,' Penny forced herself to say.

'No, you told them I was engaged to marry the patient, and they are both livid!' Belinda snapped. 'Why drag me into trouble, too?'

Penny looked as if she were going to drag Belinda into a great deal more trouble. 'See, the thing is, he made me promise to go into this for his nephew.'

There was a long silence between them, while Belinda looked at this situation in all its enormity: quite the most awful thing that Penny had done to date. No wonder she wanted to opt out of nursing!

At last, Belinda said, 'He was too ill to *make* you do anything – you know that! Just why did you get yourself into this fix? There must be more to it.'

'No, you're wrong, Bel. He *did* make me, because he was getting all upset and I said I would, hoping he'd quieten down, and he did! That's the whole point – to keep him quiet! He got all happy then and said you'd not be sorry because you'd be rich and not have a thing to worry about and–'

'No, you'd be rich,' Belinda corrected, with distaste. 'It gets worse and worse. Well, there's only one thing to do. I must go to Sister Newman with this story, which I'm sure will make her think twice about not telling the patient about the two of us, after all. I'll explain that you're the silly young sister who does mad things without meaning to make trouble, but you'll have to be there to apologise, and apologise you will, and properly! What are you shaking your head for?' Belinda broke off to ask wrathfully.

'You don't understand,' she whispered. 'I *promised!* The sort of promise you can't break, because a letter's gone to his solicitors about it.'

'What are you talking about, Penny?' Belinda asked sternly. 'How *could* he write a letter – he couldn't see!'

'I wrote it to his dictation and he managed to sign it, and the ward maid fetched a porter and they witnessed it.' Penny quailed before her sister's horror.

'Does Sister know about this?' was all Belinda could think of.

'Well, no. The girl was cleaning the floor and the porter happened to be unjamming the window. It didn't matter, did it? It's all legal now, anyway,' Penny added, half defiantly. 'He said he'd already made his Will and this was just a sort of added bit – a Coddy-something. Quite legal,' she said again, and because her sister's silence was unnerving, Penny put in for good measure, 'There's something else wrong with him and he *knows* about it and he thinks he's going to *die* and he wants all this settled up legally *right away.*'

Belinda pulled herself together. 'Well, it's got to be stopped. You're not a nurse and you'll be no good to an invalid. What's the matter with his nephew, anyway? Such a handsome young man to be an invalid!'

'He isn't handsome, not really,' Penny

mumbled unhappily.

'Don't be ridiculous. I saw the picture, didn't I?'

Penny looked as if she would like to say a lot about that, but said instead, 'He got knocked down by a hit-and-run driver and now he won't ever walk again and he hates everybody.'

'Oh, good heavens!' Belinda said faintly. 'Well, come along. I can just get hold of – now, who can I get hold of? Well, Sister, I suppose, just before she reads the Report. She won't like being held up with this sort of thing! And yes, you must come too, so no nonsense about that. Wash your face while I tidy myself, and buck up about it!'

Penny stared helplessly. 'But you don't understand!' she exclaimed, bursting into tears again. 'It's no *use* telling Sister, because the patient's *got* a proper nurse for his nephew. I *promised* – but I'd told him the name was Lulie, so he's made the arrangement in your name, and it's *you*, Bel, you will have to do it. It's no use looking at me like that. I didn't know what else to do and I couldn't call anyone. So I promised. You *will* keep the promise, won't you? I mean, I had to think quickly because he gets so upset if I don't agree and ... and...'

Before this incoherent, but still dangerous piece of intelligence, Belinda sat down limply. She should have known. Of course it

69

would be in her name. He had *called* her
Lulie, hadn't he? And he knew she was
twenty-three, a qualified nurse! Remembering that very curious conversation that day
with the patient, she now began to see what
it was about.

But one thing bothered her. 'Why should
he want me to say for sure that I was not
engaged to anyone and that the old affair was
really broken off?' she mused, half to herself.

Penny, now edging to the door, poised for
flight, said breathlessly, 'Well, it stands to
reason, doesn't it? I mean, he wouldn't want
you to be still engaged or anything, because
then you'd go off and get married and leave
his poor nephew, and he wants this to be,
well, a long-standing arrangement. Well, he
would, wouldn't he? And that's why he
made me promise...'

FOUR

She caught Penny, to take her to Sister, but
it was one thing to say they would tackle
Sister at once, but quite another thing to put
it into practice. As Belinda and the unwilling Penny approached Sister's table,
where the Report should have already been
started, it was clear that there was a flap on.

70

Penny, knowing the signs, escaped while she had a chance, and Belinda was called to help Sister in one of the side wards.

The great teaching hospitals in the capital might be able to lay on super modern Emergency Drill and equipment, but Spanwell General had no such things. It was people and their efforts, knowledge and experience who counted, at Spanwell. Sister got as many of the qualified ones around her as she could, and they coped, but when it was over, and the Report still to be read, it was clearly no time to take to Sister her trouble over Penny.

As she finally watched Sister go off duty, she thought of what she might have said, and now, with Penny gone off to safety, and only that vague story for Belinda to report, what would Sister think? Was it so bad that Belinda was committed to be a permanent nurse to a crippled patient? It might turn out that he would be brought into Spanwell, and so the patient and his uncle would have no need for all this secrecy and elaborate planning. Or ... and this was always the reaction when Belinda first heard of one of Penny's scrapes ... had she been told the whole truth?

The night crawled by. Now that Fergus Jopling's bandages had been removed from his eyes, he was no longer being specialled. At one point in the night, a junior came to her and said that Mr Jopling was asking for her, but Belinda was fixing a drip, and concentrating, and advised the junior to see if she could do something. Zoë Allen finally went into his room and settled him, as she put it.

Briefly in the quiet hour between their note taking and their routine duties, Zoë and Belinda met over cocoa in the ward kitchen. Zoë, a perpetually cheerful girl who seemed to be able to cope without any anxiety at all, said cautiously, looking steadily into her cocoa mug, 'That patient, the Jopling chappie – a bit demanding, wouldn't you say?'

Belinda's head shot up. 'Oh, yes, I meant to ask you what happened. I'm afraid I rather took it for granted that now all the flap is over and he can see, he wouldn't expect such close attention. Did you explain?'

Zoë said, 'Not exactly. Seems to me he isn't used to listening to anyone if he doesn't want to. He said he wanted you *stat*, so I said if you left the patient you were with, he would probably bleed to death. Well, even if he didn't believe me, he got the message. He said, in effect, that he wanted you for some personal thing, but he'd like a message given to you.'

Belinda looked stormy, so Zoë said, 'The message was to go to him as soon as possible. He wants to talk to you. I think maybe he decided the small hours wasn't the best time.'

Belinda hunched her shoulders. 'You

know I'm in an awful mess, and it's through Penny, as usual, but how can one allow her to get into trouble?'

Zoë said reflectively, '*You* couldn't, I could, I suppose. This wouldn't be the reason for the touching little weeping scene I broke in on, would it?'

'It would,' Belinda said grimly. 'It seems she's told him some pretty fantastic stories, and finally found he would have thought it over and decided she wasn't the person who did things for him, her only being a student. So she had the bright idea of telling him things about her (supposedly) only they were about me. So he's got a description of her and all my other details including being fully qualified, and look where that's got me! What would you do about this?' and she recounted Penny's queer story of the promise.

Zoë, who usually listened very carefully before giving a verdict, finally said, 'I don't get it, and I would suggest you ask for more details from Penny before you go to Sister or anyone else. I mean, what sort of arrangement could it be, for him to write to his solicitors about it?'

'No, it must be one of her cover-up stories. That's what I'm afraid of, really. She usually tells one yarn to blind her listener into missing the truth of the matter. She told my father that I was committed to marry the patient and not unnaturally Daddy was pretty fed up, being a doctor himself.'

'Oh, help! And word is going around that a certain person you used to know is back again, in Casualty actually. Am I treading on anyone's toes?'

'No, I would have told you myself, but things have been rather hectic lately.' She sighed and pushed her hair back. 'You know, I've never felt so beastly tired or discouraged before. It all seems to have boiled up at once.'

Zoë nodded, as if she understood. But how could she understand such a tangle, Belinda wondered, as she returned to the ward. Zoë was an uncomplicated person, from a small uncomplicated family. She had a nice tidy 'understanding' with a practical young man from home, now working at this hospital. Such a tidy existence – and she had no young sister to plague her life out. But she was a nice girl, and a good friend.

Just before dawn broke, when things were very quiet indeed and Belinda was sitting at the table with the lowered shaded light, writing up some notes, Fergus Jopling's bell went. There was nobody else on hand to go, so she went herself.

He was half sitting, leaning on one elbow, in bed, and in the half lights and softened shadows, he appeared to be more comfortable with his eyes than in the harsh light of day. He stared at her as she went over to his bedside.

'Yes, Mr Jopling, what can I do for you?' she asked softly.

'Yes, it's you all right,' he muttered, as if he wouldn't be able to be sure until he heard her voice. 'We have to have that talk, you know, and now there never seems to be an opportunity.'

'Well, let me find my friend, and warn her to keep an eye on the ward, and I'll come back for five minutes. Would you like a cup of tea? Hot milk? Anything?'

'Just that talk, and then perhaps my mind will be at rest and I shall be able to sleep,' he said, with a firmness that allowed for no argument. Well, it sounded like another thing that had been rashly promised, that talk of his. So Belinda nodded, and went to find Zoë.

Zoë was initiating a junior into how to keep awake long enough to re-stock some cupboards, and re-pack drums for the steriliser; jobs that were often done in the small hours, if and when things were quiet. They had to be done sometime by someone, and the junior had twice been discovered fast asleep over the task. Zoë left her, to go and sit at the table in the ward where Belinda had been.

Belinda herself returned to Fergus Jopling. He was waiting for her, keeping himself awake. Determined not to sleep until they talked.

'Now, Mr Jopling,' Belinda said, sitting down by him and taking one of his hands, preparing for the speech she had quickly rehearsed coming along the corridor. 'Something is worrying you and I think as you say yourself, we must have it out now. But the position as I see it is this; you were a very sick man, one who couldn't see. You have been lucky enough to have the return of the sight of your eyes but we had no certainty of that happening, and any worrying or upset might have spoilt it all, even after the operation; so we had to give in to you, anything, anything at all, in order to keep you calm and happy, until we saw if you had your sight back.'

'So you didn't mean a word of it,' he said bitterly.

'I didn't exactly say that,' she said carefully. 'What I am saying is that something is very real in your memory but it wasn't real enough for me to be able to recall what was said at this instant. But it could be real for me, if I could be refreshed. How would it be if you told me all about it, all over again?'

He looked keenly at her, but whatever he expected to see in her face wasn't there. He shrugged and said, 'Very well. I am a very rich man. I have a nephew who had a mysterious accident. I have thought all around this problem, for after I'm gone. I must be sure that the right things are done. He never was a very responsible fellow.' And remembering that handsome face in the portrait, Belinda was prepared to agree with that! 'Now, Nurse,' Fergus Jopling said, never taking his eyes from hers, 'I worked out something, which I thought – I still think – would suit all parties (and thank you for not protesting that I have an extremely good prognosis and shouldn't be worrying about when I'm gone!) but I had to have a firm and solemn promise that you would do this, just as I wanted it. That is why I required that you promised on the Bible.'

'And you think I did that?' she asked evenly, remembering he had been blind at the time.

'I know you did. I required you to fetch my own Bible from the bedside locker. I have just discovered it is still in there. I felt all over it with my fingers and discovered a familiar cut so I knew it was my Bible even though at that time I had no eyes to see with. And you promised.'

'And that,' Belinda said, her heart sinking, 'would be a promise to keep. Tell me again what it is exactly that was required of me, and don't leave a thing out, but please make it brief.'

'I will. I have arranged with my solicitors that you are not only to have my nephew's life in your hands, but my considerable private fortune. It seems reasonable, surely? But I want you to be firm with him. Don't let him organise any hair-brained schemes of revenge for what was done to him. If he wants to try more surgery, it is up to you to decide whether it is reasonable or just a pouring out of good money for no reason. There are many inventions that would be of use to him to help him to lead an interesting if not an exactly active life. And as I am convinced I shall not be here to see it, I want to start things moving now – so tell me again, Nurse, that you remember all this and that you agree you were not coerced into making such a solemn promise and that you will keep it.'

Belinda was bewildered. There was more to it, must be more to it, than this? 'Did I agree to give up my career in this hospital to go away somewhere and look after your nephew, for as long as he lived?' she asked faintly, and again the question: was it in reason that she should keep such a promise, Penny having made it? But the patient had no doubts. 'There are tremendous issues at stake and yes, you agreed to give up your career. You said it sounded utterly worthwhile and that your father, who is a G.P. would be the first to agree with you. I can't feel that you are trying to slide out of it, Nurse. Now I can see you, disappointed though I may be in the picture I was allowed to build up of you, I am quite sure that you are utterly staunch and loyal and will stand by your word in this.'

'If I gave my word, to such a matter, which

sounds rather vague, then I will keep it,' she said shortly.

The patient was leaning over the edge of the bed now, looking in his locker. 'You said, I recollect, that anyone could be a nurse in a hospital, but looking after my nephew all the time would be a real challenge. Now, Clive's address should be here and I want you to go and see him on your next time off duty. I have asked my solicitor to tell him all about this arrangement and I want you two to meet. In fact, I want you to bring him back with you for me to see. It can be arranged. His man is very efficient.'

She bent down to help him. There was the case containing the photo. She resisted the temptation to look at it again. The young man's scintillating good looks must have tempted Penny; that and his obvious wealth. And then Penny must have realised what she had done and got frightened. Scatterbrained Penny always realised she was in a mess when she was in too deep almost to get out. Belinda put the photo case on the ground, the notepaper on top of it and swiftly went through the rest of the things until she found his address book. He nodded, took it and leaned back on his pillow, exhausted. 'Look,' she said. 'Don't worry. If I made a promise in such earnest, I will keep it, don't fret. But you must get sleep now. As to going to your nephew's house; if he's coming here to the hospital, why don't I meet him here? Wouldn't that be neater all round, with such an efficient man-servant to bring him?'

'That's sensible,' the patient gasped. 'I knew you'd be all right. But I've so little time. I am so grateful to you for telling me what else was wrong with me. It gives me a chance to get my affairs in order,' he astonished her by saying.

He was tired, so she resisted the temptation to ask him just what she had said was the matter with him, tucked him down and left him, in her ears his sleepily murmured: 'You're a good girl, Lulie. I'm glad it's you!'

She was bewildered. She had had some odd patients in her time but this was the strangest. But worst of all was the thought that undoubtedly Penny must have mischievously told him what the other complication was.

Zoë Allen looked enquiringly round the door and backed out again. Belinda gave a final soft touch to his pillows and quietly followed her friend out.

'All serene?' Zoë asked, in a tone which said she knew it wasn't.

'No, far from it,' Belinda muttered. They had trained together, these two, confided in each other, shared simple harmless secrets, until Derek had come along and after Derek's brief yet devastating entry into

Belinda's life, Zoë had somehow calmed Belinda down, made her take an interest in everything again, and still kept a good friend even though she was going steady herself with a practical young man from the path lab. Logically Zoë was the person she should have told about all this, but Belinda found herself shrinking from doing so. Zoë had never understood the way Belinda and the family felt about Penny, the spoiled darling of the family, and the disruptive force among the young ones just now. But there was one thing she had to know. 'The patient thinks he's got a fatal illness, apart from his eyes. He didn't say what he thought it was. How could he have found out?'

Zoë looked really alarmed. 'Well, search me! I told you, because my Jamie told me, he being in a position to know. But he wasn't supposed to pass it on.'

'That's what I thought – about me being the only one to know, on the nursing staff that is, besides you.'

'What you mean is that your young sister Penny couldn't have known?' Zoë retorted. 'Sorry, Bel, but you and I come unstuck on that subject, don't we? Still, if you didn't tell her (and I can't see you doing such an idiotic thing) then how could she have found out?'

'I should have asked him what he meant by me telling him that,' Belinda said.

'He accused you of–' Zoë exploded, but

Belinda, following her into the kitchen said quickly, 'No, no, it wasn't like that. Actually he was thanking me for having told him that his prognosis wasn't good. He seemed glad to have the facts. No, what I was thinking was that Penny probably told him he had something else, something she'd cooked up, just to sound knowledgeable. Oh, no, she couldn't have. She wouldn't have!'

'Wouldn't she!' Zoë muttered. 'Bel, be careful of that kid. Oh, I know you don't think I like her much. It's not that. Her mischief seems harmless but one of these days it will go sour on you. It's too dangerous having someone like that, even on a very low rung of the nursing profession. I know Sister thinks she'll shape up later, but I don't, and I don't believe you do either. It's this myth having medical parents and being sure all the offspring will follow suit. They don't – well, not someone like Penny.'

Regrettably it was Belinda's inner conviction, too, but although she couldn't bring herself to say so or do anything to damage a friendship she valued, at the same time it made the words stick in her throat that would have told Zoë what else had been going on at the patient's bedside. Zoë was far too practical, sane and unimaginative to have entered into any of this from the start. Belinda was fairly sure that she would have refused to do it, even if she had been blessed with a young sister, also training to be a nurse, whose voice was sufficiently like her own to have started this rather unusual and ambitious scheme of Sister Newman's. Belinda supposed unhappily that at first the idea had seemed such a godsend and so uncomplicated, simply because Sister Newman thought she knew Penny's nature, but was really using Belinda's disposition as a yardstick, which had proved totally at fault. Belinda sighed, and put the whole thing out of her mind.

Tonight that wasn't difficult. Two emergencies came in, which made for some real excitement on the ward, at a time when there were two very ill patients at the end, and Belinda and Zoë were hard put to it to keep the ward in a quiet state while emergencies were settled in from theatre and afterwards watched. Funny, the way things flared up so suddenly.

When she finally went off duty, to a cold grey day, the day staff looked all brisk, filled with good sleep and a good breakfast, and ready for anything, while Belinda herself felt so jaded, she almost forgot that this was to be the day when she would be seeing Dr Elliott, dining with him and discussing ... oh, no! All of a sudden she felt a shrinking about telling anyone anything about this matter.

Perhaps fate taking at hand at that moment, changed everything, for young Penny skipped round a corner, laughing with another young nurse, and froze in her tracks at the sight of Belinda.

Penny! She ought to be taken to Sister, to have that talk, Belinda recalled. Penny stood frozen in front of her. The other junior basely deserted her. Here was trouble, with Belinda Fenn looking decidedly on the war path.

Penny looked at the retreating back of her companion and licked her lips. 'What are you going to do with me?' she whispered.

'You know very well I can't take you to Sister at this moment. We've had two more emergencies in!' Belinda snapped. 'But yes, there *is* something! What did you tell Mr Jopling he had wrong with him, to make him think he hadn't long to live? And I want the truth!' she added fiercely.

Penny looked scared again. 'Gosh, I hate this life. I wish I could go home,' she muttered. 'There's always something! All right, Bel, don't pinch my arm – I'll tell you! He thought I was you, all crackly with efficiency and having lots of nursing knowledge, and he asked if he had anything else wrong besides his eye thing. Golly, I couldn't remember the name of that! So to cover up, I thought up something quickly.'

'What? What did you think up?' Belinda asked tersely, unhappily aware that all this willing explanation was most unlike Penny. She must be covering up something else she'd done.

'Leontiasis ossea,' Penny said defiantly.

'What-at?' Belinda gasped. Then she felt relieved, almost ready to smile. 'Of course, he didn't believe you! He's too intelligent a man!'

'Well, he did so, and he told me he wasn't surprised because he'd been abroad and a friend of his had had leprosy and ... Bel, what is it? That thing I said he had?' Penny broke off to ask, on a sudden thought.

'Well, if you don't know what it is, where did you get hold of it?'

'At one of Dr Elliott's lectures,' Penny said simply. 'He pounced on me and accused me of not listening, and I was! I was, truly! Well, I did hear the last thing he said, and it sounded funny and it stuck in my mind and I said it, and it made the class laugh because he looked so wild because I had heard.'

'Well, you'd better go and read it up because he'll ask next time other things about it. And don't ever tell a patient he's got something unless you know what it is. The poor man must have been scared stiff at the thought of all the bones of his face getting deformed and becoming huge. Yes, that's what it is!'

'Nurse! What are you doing, still on duty?' Sister called.

'Just going, Sister,' Belinda said, but now she was even more worried. She couldn't just go and leave the patient thinking he had that disease. He might ask Sister about it, and then what would happen to Penny?

She wasn't quite sure how she was going to put it to him, but she slipped into his room, and caught him leaning over, rummaging in his locker.

'I'm just going off duty,' she said conversationally. 'I'm glad you don't really think you have any other complications, but at the same time I shouldn't lean out of bed too much, if I were you. What are you trying to reach?'

He turned and looked at her. 'Don't worry, Lulie. I won't let anyone know you were kind enough to tell me something I wanted to know very badly about my condition. And now you're here, it is most fortunate. I want you to take the photograph of my nephew, so you'll know what he looks like. Ah, yes, that's it,' and he pounced on the leather frame and opened it. 'Now, when–' he began.

She never discovered what he had been about to say. She thought she would never forget the look on his face as, opening the leather cover to reveal the picture inside, he broke off his sentence and stared with open mouth and eyes wide with incredulity and something amounting to horror.

'Mr Jopling, what is it?' she asked, puzzled.

'He – he–!' the patient stuttered, pointing a shaking finger at the photo. And then he said something that sounded like: 'Monstrous!'

and the picture fell out of his hands as he clutched at his chest, his face rigid and fell back. Running footsteps down the corridor followed close on the shout of agony torn from Fergus Jopling's lips as he collapsed.

FIVE

It seemed hours before Belinda finally left the hospital to return to the Nurses' Home and to try and catch up on her sleep. Three whole days off, before she went back to day duty, and she felt spent, ill even, and very puzzled.

That form of collapse, a cardiac collapse, was cognisant with a shock, a very bad shock. But as she had explained to Sister Newman and old Dr Harris who had been hastily called, the patient had been talking to her, pleasantly, about his nephew, just before he collapsed. She herself had gone in to see him after going off Night Duty, and he had seemed quite all right.

Yet in an odd sort of way, although the others agreed with her, Belinda had the notion that this was tied up with her young sister Penny. Penny was scared about something. Far too ready to explain things that didn't really matter, and very adept at slipping out of the explanations that Belinda really wanted.

She had a warm bath and undressed, but she could never sleep well on night duty. The sounds of Spanwell hammered at the very walls of the Nurses' Home although this building, once a tall Victorian villa in a street of such villas, was still classed as a dwelling house in a quiet side road. After an hour, Belinda gave up trying to sleep and lay there thinking.

The only key to all this was what Penny had been up to, and the only way to find that out was either to question her friends (who would clam up as Penny herself had) or to follow her, Belinda supposed.

There was, of course, the nephew being brought over to the hospital today. On that thought, she sat up suddenly in her bed. She should be around to see him, she supposed. Tell him that he couldn't see his uncle, who had been moved from his room on that floor, and taken up to the Cardiac floor. What sort of conveyance would the handsome nephew be brought in? And why had his uncle exclaimed: 'Monstrous!' about his photograph.

Belinda shook her head, but shivering, she got out of bed and dressed in warm mufti, in order to go out. She had been given the nephew's address. She could at least telephone and tell the manservant not to bring him to the hospital today.

Thinking it over, she ripped off her mufti and got into uniform. Idiot – there was still something she must do! Get that photograph from his things. He had thought she would need it and undoubtedly she would, for identification.

Sister Newman was surprised to see Belinda, but said that the patient's belongings had all been taken from his room when he had been moved to the Cardiac section. Why did Belinda want it? Belinda said, 'The patient wanted me to meet his nephew today when he was brought over to the hospital, Sister; I'd need it as I don't know him.'

'I see,' Sister Newman said slowly, staring at a picture on the wall but obviously not thinking about it. 'What were you talking to your young sister about, Nurse? You looked angry, which is not like you. And I recollect that you were bringing her towards me last evening when there was that flap on over Mr Brady.'

Sister Newman didn't miss much, Belinda thought, in dismay. But it had to be done, and in a way she was glad about it. 'It's this muddle over the two of us taking turns to be by his side, Sister,' she said, and as Sister Newman's eyebrows went up, wordlessly pointing out that that scheme was now surely passé, Belinda said diffidently, 'My sister isn't capable of not talking. She talked to the patient, but told him things about me and somehow mixed them up with things about herself. I'm afraid it's caused a bit of a muddle.'

It didn't sound very convincing but then, Belinda thought helplessly, how could she say baldly, 'My young sister told him an outrageous story about me getting involved with a property tycoon over the matter of a building containing a hairdressing saloon; she told him he had a terminal disease connected with leprosy, and she also committed me to a promise to stay with his nephew, a cripple from a car accident, for the rest of his life, in order to ensure his not indulging in wild schemes of revenge, and for which I was to inherit a sizeable fortune?' She shuddered as she heard all that in her own mind. To say it aloud would be awful.

The telephone rang and Sister paused to answer it. 'Where? Who? Well, yes, I suppose so. I'll come at once.' And she turned significantly to Belinda. 'It really doesn't sound very much out of pattern with your young sister, Nurse, and I really shouldn't get so worked up about that child if I were you. If she gets in real trouble, of course, then she will be delivered into the hands of her superiors, *stat.*' And she went out, hustling Belinda before her, clearly indicating, even if she hadn't said it, that she had enough troubles, without sorting Belinda's problems with her young sister, and looking rather satisfied that the matter would be out of her own hands and taken to higher levels.

Try as she would, Belinda couldn't see that Penny had really caused the patient to collapse. That must be something quite different he had, and nobody had realised it. Belinda rather wished that Spanwell General Hospital had the wherewithal and the people to proceed on patients as the Americans did, taking tests by separate specialists at the very start. In that way, a rich man like Fergus Jopling could have been examined by the heart men with their cardiograph paraphernalia, the liver men, the ears, nose and throat team, and so on, even looking at the condition of his bones. Such a comprehensive check-up by the experts would have made Penny's nonsense just laughable, instead of something that poor man had evidently believed.

On the way out of the hospital, Belinda saw the patient's eye consultant. Sir Maxwell looked anything but happy. Had he been called in again? Had it been in connection with that delicate operation, she wondered? No, hardly likely. But he was looking distinctly unhappy. He was, of course, hardly likely to be very happy since he was being buttonholed by his niece Hope, Belinda thought, as some people moved out of the way and she could now see who Sir Maxwell was talking to. With Hope was a young man so much like her in essential features that it was a fair guess that this was her brother, Lloyd. When Belinda had first come to the hospital, and had been enduring agonies over her love affair with Derek, she had vaguely heard things about Lloyd Kingston, but there had been no room to consider other people's troubles then. Now, as she passed them, and heard the young man's angry voice joining his sister's bored tones, Belinda felt an instinctive dislike of him, and was sorry for Sir Maxwell.

Derek was charging out of the door leading to the Casualty Department, and saw her. Time swooped backwards. How many times had she stood on this spot by the plinth of the statue to the hospital's early founder, and waited for Derek, admiring him in his (then) short white jacket. Now she looked more critically at him. Life hadn't treated him kindly. The smile he hastily produced had no real warmth in it, and there were lines in his young face, and dark smudges under his eyes. He must be still carrying the torch for the red-headed Marcia.

He stopped uncertainly, obviously feeling he must speak to Belinda. 'Hello, Lulie,' he said. Time was rolling back for him, too. He had forgotten she had said she didn't want to hear that little name any more. 'They wanted me to take up the job sooner. I needed the cash. No problem really. Didn't have time to contact you. Sorry about that.'

'No need to be, Derek. Have you heard anything from anyone about Marcia?'

His face wore a closed look. His eyes were anywhere but on hers as he denied any news of Marcia. 'Not that I'd want any, really. I'm sure she's just taken off. I mean, she's done it to me often enough, making me feel a right Charley.'

'Then you don't think it's the sort of disappearance one goes to police about?' and to her it seemed a most logical question. Derek, however, turned on her, frowning, alarmed. 'Good heavens, no, you haven't said anything to anyone about it, have you? We don't want the police contacted about this! You wouldn't would you?'

'No, but do let go of my arms, Derek. Sir Maxwell is looking very oddly over at us.'

Derek let go and nervously brushed a hand down the back of his head then abruptly left her. She made to go in the other direction, out of the hospital, when Sir Maxwell accosted her.

'Nurse!' he said. 'I wonder if you'd be kind enough to do something for me?'

'Of course, Sir Maxwell. Is it about Mr Jopling?'

'Mr Jopling?' He looked bewildered. 'Oh, heavens, no. Bad business that. I understand you were with him at the time,' so she felt she ought to give him her version again. He listened abstractedly, and finally said, 'Yes, well, he's in good hands. Gets too tensed up, Jopling. Warned him about tension. However... Oh, this thing I want you to do.' He stared at the departing backs of his niece and nephew. Morosely, he said, 'I wish you'd pop up to John and Mary Wynne Ward with this. There's a Mrs Ivory, first bed inside. I did say I'd look in on her but I can't just at the moment and I want her to have that. Would you, Nurse?'

'Of course,' Belinda said, rather bewildered. A junior or a porter could have taken it. But she didn't mind. Poor man, he didn't look very happy. She guessed it might be Hope worrying him, and considering Hope was reputed to be about to become engaged to Adam Elliott, there was another poor man she had to be sorry for. Well, she told herself fiercely, Adam Elliott didn't have to take on Hope Kingston. It wasn't as if he was married or engaged to her already. Or was it? Were there other things considered?'

She went up the three flights to John and Mary Wynne Ward. It was a terminal ward. Belinda wondered how a patient in there could have need of the eye surgeon. She had heard what a kind man Sir Maxwell was, so it was likely that he was writing to the patient about a relative with an eye condition. She looked for the ward sister, who said, 'For Mrs Ivory, Nurse? Take it to her, will you?

She's expecting it. Oh, and can you spare a minute to have a chat with her? She's a bit down this morning.'

Sister hurried away, rushed off her feet and short-staffed. Belinda looked at the first bed, expecting a very old lady. But she didn't know why. Mrs Ivory was far from old. In her middle forties, good-looking, elegant even, and vaguely reminding Belinda of someone. She went and pulled the stool out, and said, 'Hello. I'm off duty so I wondered if you'd like a few words. Sir Maxwell asked me to bring that up to you.'

Mrs Ivory smiled sweetly at Belinda and said, 'Be a dear and open it and read it, will you? I'm not seeing too well today.'

Belinda glanced up at the notes, and flushed unhappily. She should have known – of course Sir Maxwell was involved. And no wonder he was unhappy. Was this what Adam had meant when Belinda had asked if he had any failures? Was this his one failure?

She slit the envelope and got out a single sheet. 'It says: "My dear Ellen. You were right. I am less organised now, and things pile up. Forgive? I will look in, as soon as I can, and I haven't forgotten what you asked me to bring, if you really want it." That's all, actually.'

'It's a notelet?' Mrs Ivory asked. 'Would you mind describing the picture on the front? I hope it's a cat picture.'

'Oh, are you a cat-lover too?' Enthusiasm crept into Belinda's voice. 'So am I! This is rather a nice one. A really naughty kitten face peeping through a bank of flowers.'

'In a garden?'

'No, spilled from a vase on a highly polished table,' Belinda said ruefully.

A ripple of laughter came from the patient. 'I shall like that. I shall see it tomorrow when Sir Maxwell sends up his gadget.' She hesitated. 'He's so good to me. It will look awful, this gadget, but what does it matter if it helps one to see? To get pleasure from pictures like that, and to read. I've got two new books on cats, and some lovely photographs friends have sent me, all of cats. Do you have a cat? At home, I mean?'

'Oh, yes. My father's a G.P. and he has a weakness for animals as well as for people. All the strays come in.'

'You have a lovely voice. I would like to talk to you again, but of course, you have your own life and your own commitments. I wish my daughter–' She broke off, then said firmly, 'Well, I mustn't be selfish. She has her own commitments, too. And she doesn't understand that to look through a gadget with thick lens is to open up a world of delight when one is caught in bed like this.' She shrugged a little. 'My daughter thinks I should be in a side ward. She just doesn't understand – it's so lonely in there. There are people here, and something going on all the time.'

'I know,' Belinda said. 'But I'm tiring you. I think I ought to go.'

'No, don't go, not just yet. Well, unless I'm keeping you from—'

'Oh, no, you're not. I can stay another ten minutes, anyway. Oh, there is a telephone call I ought to make. No, well, it's early yet. I should think another ten minutes wouldn't hurt. No, it isn't a boy-friend,' she smiled. Then she felt cold. But it was a man she was committed to spend a life time with, wasn't it?

Mrs Ivory said, 'Tell me about yourself. You're a new person. It's fresh and interesting. You've got a problem, I can tell. Tell me about it. I always ask people for their problems. The ward maid has the most fascinating jumble of things happening in her life, but she stumbles out of the fixes somehow. What's yours?'

Belinda was tempted. Here was a complete stranger, not like Zoë who knew the people and circumstances, not like Dr Elliott who would probably frown on every aspect of this case, when she got round to telling him about it over dinner tonight. Besides, this woman was almost in a world of darkness. Perhaps she would understand.

'I'd like to tell you about it,' Belinda said suddenly. 'But of course I mustn't mention names, you understand.'

'Of course,' the patient agreed, and now her face was alive with interest.

'You see, the problem is, does this promise have to be kept? It was made by a very young nurse, to a patient, only she got scared at what she was doing, and had the bright idea of making it in the name of an older, more experienced nurse. But the patient didn't know.'

'What was the promise, or shouldn't I ask?'

'The patient had a relative who needed a nurse, permanently. The patient thought what a bright idea it would be to tie this nurse down for the lifetime of the crippled relative, so he wouldn't be left high and dry. The patient, who is rich, thought he could buy such a service with a large sum of money, when he died. And he expects the promise to be kept.'

'Does the older nurse know about it yet?' the patient asked, her lips twitching. 'My dear, I shouldn't be amused, but what fun the younger girl must be, to gaily make such a promise, then have the wit to chicken out by using someone else's name.'

Fun. Yes, they all thought Penny was such fun, Belinda thought in surprise. Penny was selfish and irresponsible and incapable of taking life seriously. She was also dead sure of someone coming to bale her out. 'The older girl knows about it, and is prepared to keep the promise as it appears to have been made on the Bible. But is it right?'

The patient thought about it then shrugged. 'Why am I hesitating? Of course it's right, as it was made in such solemn circumstances. Was the patient blind?' she asked calmly, as if her own lack of vision was something quite different.

Belinda said, unthinkingly, 'Yes, temporarily that is.' Then bit her lip. That would have completely betrayed who it was. 'I see you guess the identity. Can I ask you not to mention it to a soul?' she asked urgently.

'Yes, you can, my dear, and you need have no fear, I assure you. Sir Maxwell isn't blind, however, although he doesn't appear to notice much, and yes, I think that promise will undoubtedly have to be kept. Perhaps it's as well,' she said, obscurely.

'What made you say that?' Belinda asked, getting up to go, and wishing she hadn't mentioned the matter at all.

'Well, the older nurse may feel that she's the prisoner of a promise, but taking things all round, she may be rather glad of the compulsion behind it. She may not know, for instance, that Dr Elliott isn't free. He's a prisoner, too, of a kind, and not at all the sort of man to break his bond, either.'

Belinda thanked the ward sister for letting

her stay, and the ward sister in turn thanked her for giving her time. 'That patient is a most tragic case,' she mused, as she walked a little way down the corridor with Belinda. 'It should never have happened. But there, there's nothing that can be done for her. And she is such a brave soul, and such a nice woman to know. Tragic, all round.'

Clearly Belinda wasn't expected to ask in what way Mrs Ivory was tragic, so she went, still filled with her own thoughts about the tangle of her life at the present moment. As if she had thought there would be a chance to break that promise, or even that she would *want* to! But she sincerely hoped that Penny would never make another promise in her name.

She hurried to find a phone to call up Clive Gregory's home to tell him about his uncle, but when she got through to switch-board, they said, 'No need to get through to the Gregory house, Nurse. He's here.'

'Here! Already?'

'Yes, well, fact is, he seems to have had a spot of bother on the way. Got mixed up in an accident on the way and brought in a bit shaken up. Bad-tempered young bloke, isn't he, Nurse?'

'Well,' Belinda said with some asperity to the porter, 'he is, after all, a permanent cripple. It can't have been much fun being in another accident. I must come down to see him.'

'Well, you'll find him sitting there in a wheel chair, all waiting, Nurse, and rather you than me,' the switchboard operator said.

Belinda hurried down to Casualty. Derek would no doubt have the case in hand, she thought.

Another lot of ambulances were coming in, and Casualty staff moved over to the doors. Belinda looked round at the faces of people waiting. Casualty patients she had noticed before, tended to have a set blank look on their faces. No interest, even in the fact that three or four ambulances were noisily pro-claiming they had brought in urgent cases from some drama outside the hospital walls. The only face with any liveliness in it was the one she sought. The improbably handsome young man in the photo in Fergus Jopling's locker. There he was, in his wheel chair, looking over to the doors with a great deal of lively interest. Well, that was gallant for someone permanently crippled in one acci-dent and already in another, she thought, as she briskly went across to him.

'Mr Gregory? Mr Clive Gregory?' she asked, just to make sure. 'I am–' she began, but the good-looking young man laughed and said, 'No, love, don't look all upset over me. I'm really not supposed to be in this thing but the fact is, it looked less uncom-fortable than those benches. I'm actually waiting to go in to see Sir Maxwell. His clinic is today, I believe.' And he casually lifted his length out of the wheel chair and stood looking down at her, amusement still glinting in his face.

'You're *not* Mr Jopling's nephew?' She couldn't believe it.

'No, but I almost wish I were, if it were to get me all that anxiety and interest from that lovely face, Nurse!' and he touched her chin with a tentative finger. 'Skin like velvet,' he murmured. She shrank away from him.

Another nurse who had skimmed by, came back. 'You want Mr Jopling's nephew, Fenn? Over in the end cubicle, and rather you than me!' and she went to help the people round the last ambulance.

Now Casualty was uncomfortably full. Belinda hurried over to the last cubicle, where a young man lay on the couch. He turned a dark sullen face to hers. Bad-tempered, Penny had called him. But how had she known? She had only seen the photo of the handsome young man who wasn't crippled. And come to think of it, how was it his picture had been in the leather case, and not this one, which undoubtedly must have been the one Penny saw?

The young man said, in a surly voice, 'Don't tell me someone's come for me at last!' and he tried to reach a briefcase on the chair by him. He made an imperious gesture so she automatically gave it to him. He pulled out a photo and studied it. 'Oh, yes, you're the one my uncle wanted me to look out for,' and he didn't seem pleased.

She leaned over and saw with shock that he had a picture of herself. One recently taken for her father. She reddened as she again recognised Penny's hand in all this. Only Penny could have known where to put her hands on that picture and she must have given it into the patient's hands to send to his nephew before he regained his sight, as Fergus Jopling hadn't recognised her.

Clive Gregory was to go up to the wards. Belinda set about his removal on Derek's instructions. Derek didn't like the surly patient, either. Then as Belinda and a porter began to push the trolley towards the lifts, she saw the handsome young man again, emerging from Sir Maxwell's room. Already? Long before the clinic had started? And such a short consultation? To her surprise the young man was casually tucking what appeared to be bank notes into his breast pocket.

SIX

Belinda stared at Adam Elliott. He looked rather different in mufti, much nicer, she thought. A rush of warmth went over her. She made up her mind on the instant that she would tell him everything. Here he was asking her, not for the first time, to unload on to his broad and capable shoulders, and the temptation was too much for her.

He had brought her to this restaurant, in a favourite hotel of his. Near at hand the sea washed lazily on the shore. Cheppingstock wasn't a popular seaside resort so it was quiet outside. Evening meant, in this place, people quietly strolling, and relaxing; soft music coming out from restaurants whose clientele didn't want the more popular or stirring sounds. The day-time blare of traffic had subsided. The flower-edged road by the sea-front was almost deserted of cars. A peaceful place, the sort of place Adam would bring someone to. Someone? Why wasn't it Hope Kingston with him this evening, Belinda suddenly wondered?

Adam finished ordering, tasted the wine with due ceremony, waited till the first course was brought, then smiled encouragingly at her. 'As a poker player, you'd be a washout,' he told her. 'You've already decided to tell me everything, then altered your mind, while I've been ordering. Now what made you do that?'

She was surprised, put out by such perspicacity, yet oddly pleased. He noticed things about a girl, and that was nice. Derek never noticed what she was feeling. *He* just wanted rapt attention reflected in her face while he talked of himself. He hadn't changed much now, she thought, remembering the few minutes he snatched to speak to her in Casualty today, presumably to ask why she had looked so upset over the intake of Clive Gregory, but terminating briskly into a quick opportunity to tell her that he had had no news of Marcia and confiding his fears about Marcia's safety and trying at the same time to enlist Belinda's personal help in finding Marcia.

Belinda said, 'I'm torn in so many ways,' with a sigh that almost took her own appetite away. The soup was good and thick and inviting, but she didn't want to eat. 'Can I ask you a question, and you just say yes or no, instead of asking me how the situation came about?' she asked, all in a rush.

He looked faintly alarmed. 'No,' he said uncompromisingly. 'At least, you can ask it, but I can't and won't promise just to say yes or no, without knowing what the issue is.

You must know I would say that.'

Of course she knew. He was an honest man and no fool. She had known that the first moment she had ever set eyes on him and that was a good while ago. He had been growing on her, she thought, in sudden alarm. Growing on her because she was ripe for someone to do that, to fill the gap that Derek (or the dream image of Derek) had left when he had gone. 'Yes, well, it would get my sister Penny into trouble, I'm pretty sure.'

'Oh, I knew that,' Adam said easily, and put his hand over her smaller one. 'Where's that courage of yours? Go on, tell me all about it.'

She hesitated, remembering the patient in the Terminal Ward this morning, asserting with apparent irrelevancy, that Adam was committed, not free. Well, it didn't mean to say she was going to try and steal him, did it, or break up his near engagement with some other girl just by doing as he suggested, and telling him what the trouble was – especially as it concerned a patient of his.

'Well, I tell you what,' he said, before she could speak. 'I've finished my soup and you haven't, so why don't I ask you questions, relevant questions, and you can just answer yes or no? Well, the answers might be somewhat longer, but at least I'll let you know what I want to know, or to be clear on. Go on!'

She nodded, helplessly.

'Right, then for a start, what was the significance of your looking horrified at a new intake in Casualty this afternoon?'

'It was Clive Gregory, the crippled nephew of Fergus Jopling,' she said baldly.

'That is his identity. What was the significance of your horror?'

'It's a long story,' she said, abandoning the excellent soup because the waiter was hovering, worried about the cooling of the next course. Her soup was whipped away, and the next course served, but although she gained time through this, it didn't give her an indication of how to answer, how to wriggle out of the hole she was in.

'Well, I must know it, and tonight. I have one of those impending doom feelings,' Adam said cheerfully. 'Don't kill me with suspense!'

'Oh, Doctor Elliott!' she protested, thinking he was laughing at her.

'*Adam,* or I won't let you finish this excellent meal. I shall take you back to the hospital unfed and probably by then very hungry. And your name, I gather, is Bel. At least, that is what I've heard your young sister call you.'

'The family call me Bel, short for Belinda.'

'Then, Bel (which is a very beautiful name and quite suits you) how come I distinctly heard the patient, on several occasions, refer to you as Lulie?'

'I don't know,' she said at last, after a stricken look at him. 'I don't believe my young sister told him. She couldn't have known it. It was the name ... a former man-friend gave me. A long time ago. When Penny was still a schoolgirl.'

'All over now?' he asked sympathetically.

She nodded. All over, dead, but haunting her because Derek had come back.

'So, Bel, that is Mystery No. 1. Now, the nephew – I understand he was crippled in a road crash, but was being brought to the hospital today to see his uncle, didn't know his uncle had collapsed, and got caught up in another road crash – poor devil. How much did you know about that?'

'Very little. I feel as if I've been fed bits of this, over the last few days, and it's a bit of a muddle in my head,' she admitted. 'The biggest muddle was what the patient's nephew looked like. I honestly thought he was the handsome young man in the photo-graph – the one the patient was holding when he collapsed. But it wasn't him at all.'

Now Adam wasn't making any attempt to eat but was sitting quietly watching her, listening intently, thinking about what she said. 'I just don't understand any of it,' she burst out suddenly, putting down her knife and fork. 'You see, my sister Penny saw the photo of his nephew first, and she must have said he was bad-tempered. (She admitted as much to me later). The patient put the photo in my hands and asked me to repeat what I thought of him (could it have been because he wasn't satisfied and wanted to catch me out?) and at that stage I didn't know about what Penny's opinion had been. I answered as I thought she would – an incredibly good-looking young man so I said he was "super-duper". Well, Penny's type of answer. Mr Jopling seemed distinctly disappointed and said it wasn't what I'd said the day before, and of course, later, when I questioned Penny, she admitted she'd come out bluntly with the fact that he looked bad-tempered.'

'Well, I think that's a fair description of the young man I went purposely to meet this afternoon,' Adam agreed.

'Yes, but the whole point is, the man I saw the photo of, was in a wheel chair. Mr Jopling told me before his collapse that he had arranged for his nephew to be brought to the hospital to see him, but finally agreed with me that as he was coming to the hospital anyway, I could surely meet him on his arrival. Then Mr Jopling collapsed, but when I phoned down to the switchboard to try and stop the nephew coming, the porter said, "Too late, he's here – he's been in an accident himself and is sitting in a wheel chair waiting for you" so I went down. And there was this very good-looking young man

I'd said was "super-duper" in the photo.'

Adam nodded, waiting silently, so she continued, 'I asked him if he was Clive Gregory,' and she recounted what had happened then, putting in perhaps more detail than she would have otherwise, because now it had come to the painful point of telling Adam everything, she wanted him to have as accurate a picture of this bewildering situation as possible.

'Another nurse I knew went by, and came back. She must have heard me ask if he was Clive Gregory, because she said Clive Gregory was in the end cubicle. It was a bad shock, I can tell you! And yes, I found him to be a very sullen-looking young man.'

'That's just how I should describe him. Dark hair, dark grey eyes, very angry-looking,' Adam said, and Belinda agreed. 'What happened then, Bel?'

'He was grumbling at being kept waiting and he was trying to reach a briefcase. I gave it to him and he got out a photo and looked at it. It was one of me!'

'A photo of you! How did he get hold of that?'

'His uncle had sent it for identification, he said. Mr Jopling must have got it from Penny. Nobody else could have known about it, because I'd had it taken recently, expressly for my father. A birthday present. He's not an easy man to choose presents for, and I knew he wanted my picture,' she said, angrily.

Adam Elliott looked as cross as Belinda, at the thought of a photo of her being given to a strange young man. 'What happened to the other chap, the one you had thought was the nephew?' he asked suddenly.

'That's the odd thing about it. He didn't leave the hospital. He said he was waiting for Sir Maxwell's eye clinic and checked with me that it was that day. But when I was accompanying Clive Gregory on the stretcher to the lifts, I saw him leave Sir Maxwell's door, and go towards the outer door to leave. He couldn't have been in there above a few minutes.'

'That's a much better lead!' Adam exclaimed. 'So Sir Maxwell will know who he is. Right, let's see–' He consulted his watch. 'Too soon to catch Sir Maxwell. We'll give him another half an hour. Then all we have to do is to phone and ask the patient's name, and that should lead us to the answers to a number of questions.'

'Like for instance how his photo came to be in the leather case on which was written a greeting from his nephew to his uncle?'

'Now that's different,' Adam said slowly. 'Written on the photo?'

'No! Written on the transparent plastic sheet the photo was slipped behind.'

'Oh. I see.' But he didn't see. It was at best a senseless business, one designed, it seemed, to upset a patient they had been falling over backwards by unceasing strategies to keep calm and happy. 'Look, eat your food, Bel. You look as if you need it. And while you're eating, I'll tell you what I know. It isn't just what you've told me but what I've discovered by listening to other people.' He smiled lop-sidedly. 'Not eavesdropping. Just training myself to listen and watch. A patient is surrounded by problems. We are not here just to heal his body. We must often find out what ails him in his mind before we can heal his body.'

Belinda nodded. This was a familiar axiom. She had heard it at home. Her father unceasingly studied his patients, mentally as well as physically. She did her best to eat, so that Adam would get on with revealing what he had found out. She was rather shocked to think he knew so much.

'Your young sister Penny talks at top rate to her friends, oblivious of the fact that older members of the hospital staff are not deaf or stupid. I don't think she's consciously in trouble. I think she falls into it naturally like a puppy, and twists and wriggles to get out. Desperate to get out, and doesn't really realise how she is dragging others into trouble – you, for instance.'

Belinda was not happy. He continued, 'There is this business of the patient knowing what else was wrong with him.'

'Oh, that!' Belinda exploded, and told him what her sister had said about that.

He looked rather taken aback. 'Well, be that as it may, he clearly didn't believe that that was what was ailing him. My guess is that he thought you were fobbing him off out of kindness, and he guessed what his malady really was. I wonder if he knew he had a heart condition too?' He frowned. 'We could have coped with one or the other. The drug he was having for the disease he caught on his travels was just beginning to bite. We could have coped with that. Or we could have coped with his heart condition. Both at the same time, well–!'

She nodded. 'I've kept asking how he is, but they won't tell me. "Holding his own" is for relatives. Not for someone on the staff. Why don't they let me know?'

There was a silence, then he said quietly, at last, 'According to the nephew, you are more involved with the family than if you were just staff.'

She stared at him, puzzled, unable to see the significance behind his remark. Finally, she said, 'I know of nothing else than this promise.' She put her hands to her head. 'It's getting out of all proportion. The stupidest thing – a prank of Penny's – and yet, it can't be swept aside like that. I've got to keep it. For one thing, it involves a qualified nurse (which Penny isn't) and the ability to handle all that money, which Penny hasn't got. She's too young, anyway, and I'm not even sure that I have the ability. But more than all that, there's the question of honour. The promise was made, and it's got to be kept by someone. Besides, it's a legal matter now, because he dictated a letter to Penny to write to his solicitors, and he signed it. A sort of codicil to his Will. It's final, and that's why, I suppose, the nephew looks on it as involvement.' But clearly Adam didn't see it that way at all.

'If it had been anyone else,' he said, 'I would have agreed with that.'

'Then why don't you agree with it, in any case?'

Obviously unwillingly, he said, 'Bel, is there anything else you have to tell me about this queer business? I know it was an unfair pressure on you, having your sister (who is such a talkative young lady) in that room with the patient, telling him heaven knows what fairy stories, to pass the boring hour or so. But there must be some way you could have talked to the patient–'

'To make him realise that I have silly patches and I'm not responsible? I tried that. He said he liked my giddy moods but he knew that the real me was the serious one. I sometimes wonder if he knew all the time that there were two of us – he's an intelligent man. He could have got his own way by pretending not to know, couldn't he?

114

He must have known there were two of us. He held Penny's hand sometimes. He held mine, too. I held his once when he was upset. I would have thought a man would know the difference between the touch of one woman's hand against another. Would you know, Dr Elliott?'

'*Adam,* and yes, I would know,' he said quietly, with such an intent look that she couldn't meet it and dropped her own eyes in puzzled confusion. He was just saying that to prove a point, she told herself fiercely, remembering what Mrs Ivory had said. And Mrs Ivory's other remarks seemed to have some significance. She said thinking, 'Anyway, I'm a prisoner of a promise, Mrs Ivory said.'

'Mrs Ivory? What's she got to do with it?' he asked sharply.

'Sir Maxwell asked me to take up a note for her this morning. He'd promised her a contraption to enable her to see a bit. She's got a cat book and pictures she wants to look at. She asked me to stay and talk to her, so I – I thought it might be a good idea to ask her that question, about if I had to keep the promise. Only I didn't tell her any names. Well, it seemed a good idea, her being a stranger. One can't ask one's best friend, without telling her the whole miserable story. My best friend is much too practical and uncomplicated to understand how a young sister can

115

get me into such difficult positions.'

'And what did Mrs Ivory say?'

'She said yes. She was the one who coined the phrase "a prisoner of a promise" and it's stuck in my mind and keeps popping up. I don't know why I bothered you with it. It's cut and dried, isn't it?'

'Is that all you wanted me for: to answer a question, Bel?'

She couldn't stop her cheeks growing hot, and she couldn't meet his eyes as she said rather incoherently, 'No, not exactly. I wanted to talk to you. Friendship – well, no, I can't claim that – only it seemed to be what you were offering me. I'm an idiot. I shouldn't have thought – expected–'

'Bel, if only that sister of yours hadn't got you in this mess! I would have been so happy to– Bel, we've got to get you out of it, and we can! What are we thinking of? We'll have to be firm with Sister Newman, and make her release us from that ridiculous situation where the patient couldn't be told there were two of you. And then we must ask him why he wanted you, particularly you, to be tied down for life. There's no sense to it! Heavens, a man as rich as he is could procure the best nursing staff and other staff for his nephew, without making this absurd promise business. Leave it to me, Bel. I'll see to it.'

'But Penny promised on the Bible and used my name!' she reminded him.

116

'Which makes it all the more ridiculous,' he said impatiently. 'When the patient realises she's so young, and rather frightened, with the weight of a secret (the two of you doubling as one) he'll understand and release you. And he'll have to be persuaded to tell us what he's written to his solicitor, and to undo that.'

Belinda really felt as if a load had rolled off her shoulders. 'It's not that I'm shirking anything, but I wanted to continue in hospital, not give up hospital and be bogged down in private nursing with a young man who will be a spoiled and bitter invalid for, probably, fifty or sixty years, in some dark and dull house. Is that awful of me?'

'Awful to want to do real nursing, helping loads of people all day and every day, against one rather sullen young man who might or might not be able to discover surgical relief so he can get about again?'

'That's another thing. His uncle wants no more surgery. He said, too, that his nephew had had a mystery accident and was bent on revenge against the hit-and-run driver and I'm supposed to discourage or stop that.'

'And we want a nice clear picture of it all, and not this awful muddle of odd facts which don't fit,' Adam growled.

He signalled to the waiter to remove their plates and to bring over the trolley of delectable sweet dishes. 'To tempt your appetite and continue cheering you up,' he said. And then his smile froze.

Hope Kingston was coming across to him, threading her way through the other diners' tables, a broad and confident smile on her face, though even at this distance, her eyes looked rather cold and angry. Behind her was a young man who looked very much like her. These were the two who had been talking to Sir Maxwell only this morning.

Adam got to his feet, but he looked frankly nettled. 'Hope? You here?' he said.

'Well, of course I'm here, Adam darling. I was supposed to be your guest, remember? I always dine out on this particular night of the week because there's no one at home, and tonight because you didn't show up, I had to be taken by my dear brother. Lloyd, don't stand staring, do for heaven's sake speak to Adam!'

Lloyd Kingston said, 'Why the hell should I? He let you down tonight, didn't he?' but Hope merely laughed. 'Lloyd's in a foul mood because Uncle got wild with him and stopped his allowance. Well, what are we standing for? Lloyd, tell the waiter to bring our drinks over to Adam's table now we've found him.'

'Hope, can't you see I have a guest?' Adam said painfully. 'It wasn't tonight I was to call for you, anyway.'

'It's all right, darling,' Hope said placatingly. 'I've had your horrible cousin Oswald with me all the afternoon and he was telling me about this relative of yours you're stuck with. Oh, this would be the relative–?' and she broke off to look doubtfully at Belinda. 'Funny, Oswald gave me the impression that your relative was a bit older. Oh, well. Aren't you going to introduce us?'

Belinda put her napkin on the table and got up. 'I have to go, Dr Elliott,' she said quietly. 'Thank you for the advice. I'll speak to the patient, too.'

'No, don't go. You've no transport. I'll settle the bill and come–' but Belinda shook her head and left, while Hope purposefully held on to Adam's wrist. 'Darling, can't you see she wants to get away. Probably got a boyfriend waiting to give her a little more fun than talking about a patient over a meal in a place like this. Oh, yes, it'll be the Casualty Officer. I remember hearing someone say that girl's romance with him is on again. I wondered where I'd seen her before.'

Adam furiously removed her hand from his wrist. 'Excuse me, Hope. I'll be back. There's something I must do,' and he strode between the tables, out of the dining-room, just in time to see Bel come out of the Ladies' Room with her coat. 'Bel, one moment, please!' he said. He looked furious, so she waited.

'Even if other people are not minding their manners, there was no need for you to get up and leave so abruptly; what do you think I felt like?'

'In the ordinary way I wouldn't have,' she said painfully. 'But when Miss Kingston had been talking for a bit, I suddenly remembered what Mrs Ivory said today.'

'What the devil has Mrs Ivory got to do with it?'

'Nothing really, except that in between the other things she said, she just seemed to slip in the remark that Dr Elliott was committed already. I've been trying all day to see what she meant, but of course, I forgot Sir Maxwell's niece. I'm sorry, I shouldn't have accepted your invitation to dinner. You meant well.'

'I don't know what you're talking about! I have a perfect right to ask you to dinner with me. At least, I thought I had, but now I begin to wonder, after what Hope just said. Why the devil didn't you tell me about the new Casualty Officer, before it got too far?'

SEVEN

Useless to try and tell him, in that small space of time and that far from private place, that Derek was no longer the man in her life. Besides, there was the odd business

120

of that note which Derek still seemed to think she had sent, sending for him to come to see her. Had Hope Kingston heard that story from someone? Had that imp Penny got hold of the story? But only Derek knew about it. Surely he wouldn't have told anyone, in Penny's hearing?

Adam Elliott watched the frustrated Belinda walk away, so he hurried after her and called a taxi for her. 'This isn't the end, Bel. I have a lot to talk about with you, important things. Next time we'll go somewhere where we will be really private.'

Belinda said nothing, and she was relieved to be at last on her way back to the hospital; free to flay herself with angry thoughts, because she had succumbed to going out to dinner with Dr Elliott because she wanted to, and after Mrs Ivory had said (with some truth and inside knowledge, it seemed) that Sir Maxwell's niece was the person in Dr Elliott's life. Well, no, she hadn't said that, had she, but everyone else had named Hope Kingston as the person he was interested in, and Mrs Ivory had said, with telling brevity, that he simply wasn't free. Was it intended as a warning to a little nurse like Belinda, who might have been seen and talked about already, as having had many talks with him, and been given a lift at the bus stop by him. The fact that they had merely discussed a patient, meant little or nothing to those people who wanted, undoubtedly, to see a match between Sir Maxwell's niece and the up-and-coming Dr Elliott.

Derek was going off duty when Belinda got back to the hospital. She was in no mood to talk to him. He waited till she paid off her taxi, then said, 'Lulie, I've got to talk to you. No, it's not about Marcia. I've heard nothing about her – that chap I was to meet didn't turn up. No, it's about the patient today. What made you look like death when you went into the cubicle? Did you know him?'

'Derek, I can't stop now. There's something I must do. It's a matter of a photo, and the patient Fergus Jopling, the casualty's uncle. I must hurry.'

'Photo? The one they found under the bed when the nurses started to clean out his room? Oh, that's old hat. It's found, because Jopling was yelling for it.'

Belinda stopped, her hand dashed to her mouth. 'What happened? Did he have another heart attack?'

'Heavens, no. He's not doing so badly considering,' Derek said easily. 'And it seemed it's the picture he was wanting.'

'But how can that be? The picture that upset him was–' she began, then bit her lip. There was no point in telling yet another person about the wrong photo.

'Go on,' Derek invited, taking her arm.

She didn't want him to take her arm, but

she hadn't the heart to shake off his hand. 'No, as you say, it's all right only I can't believe it's ended so well,' she said quickly. 'Tell me about you. Are you settling in all right? Like the job?'

He shrugged. 'As much as I'll ever like any hospital job.'

'I expect you're missing Marcia. Have you been to the police, Derek?'

'No. I can't believe anything bad has happened to her. Besides, I know her moods too well. She probably took off because I got ratty with her. Well, you know what it's like when one's worried about where the next job is going to turn up and you know me – never could make ends meet. I suppose that's it. I got sore with her. I expect one of these days she'll either turn up or she'll send me a line and I'll know it's on again. Meantime, there's you.'

'Afraid not,' Belinda said tautly, shocked that he could so easily assume that she was there for the taking. 'Actually, Derek, there's someone else. Really there is. Sorry, but there it is. Hope your Marcia turns up soon.'

Derek was a sore loser. 'Well, if it's Elliott you're after, he's booked – by Sir Maxwell's niece. Hope Kingston. And if any gossip suddenly piles up about you, don't say I didn't warn you. Hope has got her claws in him and she won't let go, and I hear she's not a clean fighter.'

'Why don't you wait for me to say it's Dr Elliott?' Belinda said angrily. 'I haven't, you know. I haven't mentioned him.'

She left Derek looking rather uncertain, and went into the Nurses' Home to change out of her good clothes into something comfortable. Now she was back in her own room, she remembered the wave of excitement she went out on, earlier this evening. Useless to try to suppress it. And now there was nothing. But ... the matter of the photo was cleared up, apparently.

But how? The question hit her like a physical thing. How had she let herself be persuaded that it was all satisfactory? It wasn't. She was still tied to that promise, and if Dr Elliott was as tied to Hope Kingston, then what did either he or Belinda herself think he could do about the whole miserable business? Hope Kingston wouldn't let him free for one minute, now she had seen him taking a nurse out to dinner. Cold hatred had been in Hope's eyes tonight, which had made Belinda lose her nerve, and get up to go. It had been the most awful situation. Well, Adam Elliott couldn't help, so there was only one person who could: Penny.

Pausing with the zip of her best dress undone, Belinda decided that now was the moment. The little wretch would just about be returning to the juniors' floor, supper over and everyone ready to start doing things they liked instead of getting down to study. Belinda decided, zipped up her dress again, and shot downstairs to Penny's floor. Penny's door was open, but her best friend Jill Metcalfe was coming out, and looked distinctly guilty when she saw Belinda.

'Penny's not here,' she said quickly. 'I've just been looking in her room for her.' A cursory glance on the part of Belinda verified that that was true.

'Just a minute. You'll probably do,' Belinda said, with no great warmth in her voice, for although Jill Metcalfe didn't look much like Tess Upcroft, there was a family likeness somewhere, perhaps in the inquisitive stare, the quick cunning look that brought the instant decision to talk fast and sidle off out of trouble. Belinda didn't like her but she must get some answers from someone. 'Where did Penny get the real photo for Mr Jopling? She must have been the one. The real photo wasn't in the case earlier.'

Something flared in Jill's face and was quickly smothered. 'I don't know what you're talking about,' she said woodenly, adding, for good measure, 'Honestly!'

'Then go and find my sister Penny and I intend to wait here till you do. Right – you don't know where she is, so go and look for her! And bring her here fast!'

The telephone rang. Jill paused, wanting badly to answer it. Perhaps it was a call they expected. Belinda said, with the weight of her seniority, 'Get moving! I'll answer the telephone!' and she went over and lifted the instrument down.

'Nurse Fenn here,' she said, and waited.

A man's lazy voice answered. 'Hoity-toity, Nurse Fenn indeed! Now what sort of tricksy new mood is this, little Penny?'

Belinda gripped the receiver, all her senses on the alert. This was no boy who was ringing Penny up, with such casual assurance that told her it was no new friendship. This was a man, a self-assured man. But who?

'Who am I speaking to?' she asked. Well, their voices were alike, she supposed, and the man must have been used to Penny's tricks, for he laughed, an irritated laugh albeit, but he did say, rather impatiently, 'Okay, you want to play games, love. Let's get it over with, then. This is Gilbert Orr Esquire for Nurse Penelope Fenn. And is he speaking with Penny Fenn? Okay, then love, listen and listen good. I've been doing a lot of thinking, and I want *out*. You're too young and too tricky, and a bit more of your nonsense, and I'll have someone call up your superiors. Okay, you think I'm playing dirty, but I told you all along I am not used to nursery dates. I'm a big man, and I'm tired of all this.'

Belinda got her breath back. 'Really,' she said coldly. 'I'm glad to hear it put so concisely. This is not Penny but her elder sister and I believe I know just who Mr Gilbert Orr is!' she said shortly. 'And I hope you really mean it's ended!'

The last thing Belinda wanted was for that man to be ringing up to make trouble for Penny. As she replaced the receiver, Jill Metcalfe came scurrying along the passage, a very white-faced Penny in tow. 'Was that call for me?' she jerked out.

'In there,' Belinda said sharply, pointing to Penny's room. 'You, too, I think,' she said, not because she wanted Jill Metcalfe in on the conversation but because Jill Metcalfe seemed to be so anxious to get away. It could be she was in this just as much as Penny.

'Sit down,' Belinda said, but the younger ones both refused to. Aggravatingly they stood to attention, just as if Sister were questioning them. So Belinda said firmly, 'Okay, if that's the way you want it! I want answers, truthful answers, and now. If not, I take you both to Sister and I don't have to tell you who *she* will take you to, and I mean that!'

Penny wriggled, her mind working at a frantic rate. But although she seemed to be glad her friend was there by her, for some reason Jill Metcalfe wasn't so keen. Finally she gulped and said, in a rather loud voice, 'I won't do it. I won't stand by you, Pen! It's all very well for you – your father says you can leave, at once if you want to. But I can't reach my people. I've *got* to stay on here, and I'm not going to carry the can for you.'

'But you promised!' Penny wailed.

'You and your promises! You don't keep them. And I'm not going to. I dare not. Don't you see?'

'Just a minute,' Belinda broke in. 'When did Daddy say you could leave?'

Penny looked sullen. Jill answered for her. 'Yesterday. She's been on the phone home every day pestering her parents. I don't care, Pen – you let me down and I'm not going to stand by you any more. It's a silly mess, anyway.'

'You've been worrying Daddy, and he's not well?' Belinda was so angry. But she calmed down, recollecting what she had to find out at this moment, and anyway, she could tackle her sister about her father in private. 'Meantime, just why aren't you so sure of being able to leave, young lady?' she demanded of Jill.

'Because my home's shut up. My people are abroad.'

'And what about your cousin, Tess Upcroft?'

Jill's face stained a deep red, then whitened. 'Well, that's the whole point,' she said, gulping. 'I mean, everyone's got to look after themselves. It's a rotten world, and Tess is trying to get a resident nursing job and–'

'And she muscled in on this business of Fergus Jopling and his horrid nephew,'

Penny said, flashing a triumphant glance at her friend, who wasn't going to mention that. 'Well, she sent in *her* photo so I sent yours. I sent mine, too, for good measure, only he sent it back and said he didn't want a little doll.' She looked mulish, then she started to laugh. 'What do I care? I'm out of it all. I never did want to be anyone's nurse.'

'You really are the end,' Belinda said softly. 'How dare you send a photo of mine, one I had taken specially for Daddy?'

'Well, I asked him if I could. Well, he said anything was better than–' but here she looked uncertain and broke off quickly.

'Better than what?' Belinda demanded.

Jill was about to cut in, so to stop her, Penny said, 'The thing is, people shouldn't be so soppy wanting photos of nurses. There's a proper way of going about it. You go to the Thingummy of Private Nurses – a Bureau or something, like an Employment Agency, and you do it all above board. Well, Mr Jopling's nephew didn't so he was asking for people to lark about with photos.'

Jill, bitter now, said, 'You're the end to talk about larking with photos, after what you did about the other one.'

'Oh, yes, the photo of Clive Gregory. Was that your work, Penny?' Belinda asked.

Penny looked as if she wasn't going to answer, decided that nothing could touch her now as she was leaving the hospital, and brazened it out. 'Yes, I did. Well, what else could I do? I split my tea all over the soppy photo and he *was* bad-tempered in the picture, like I said. Well, I knew Mr Jopling would want to keep getting it out and you could feel the stain all rough where it dried, so I asked Jill for another photo the same size and she was the one who got it.'

Jill seemed about to protest, but Belinda cut her short. 'How? And who was it in the picture?' so Jill scowled and said, 'It was your Penny's fault. She said she'd tell on me for coming in after hours one night so I had to. It was only a spare, lying around in Unwin's father's studio.'

'Unwin?' Belinda queried, so Penny leapt in. 'Unwin Calder, who's father's got a studio in the town, and the chap in the photo couldn't collect it because he hadn't paid his bill and nobody wanted it and nobody would have found out only you had to go and say how handsome he was.'

'Haven't you two heard of deceit, and cheating and things like that?' Belinda said acidly, but Penny smartly said, 'You did as much as we did, you know you did! You could have told him you didn't make that promise!'

'I was carrying out orders, and trying to shield you from whatever you'd been doing!' Belinda said painfully, but Penny, not at all contrite, said, 'And I was carrying out orders, too, letting the patient have his own way.'

'And you were still doing that when you put back the original photo?'

'Well, he can see now, and I did rather hope to get it back before he got a sight of it and I think I did!' She wavered as Jill, shaking her head madly, kicked her. 'Well, didn't I?' Penny asked her friend uncertainly.

Belinda said, 'No, you didn't. He saw that picture, stared at it in horror and then collapsed. Oh, I don't suppose the picture made him do that, though who are we to say? We don't know what else was in his mind or what the picture meant to him, and you haven't told me who it is who didn't pay his bills so his photo was lying around for brats like you two to make mischief with.'

Jill went sullen. 'I don't know who it is. I expect Unwin's father would only he doesn't know about all this and Unwin said not to tell him or there'd be trouble.'

'So – all because of spilling tea over a photograph and not owning up, all this trouble has been caused!' Belinda said scathingly. 'And while I'm on the subject, why did you tell him about going to a property tycoon about a hairdresser?'

Belinda thought her young sister was about to faint. Jill, to get her own back no doubt, looked pleased to be able to say, 'She did it for a dare! We all do!' she added handsomely.

'You mean … you *did* go? It wasn't just a story to amuse the patient?'

She could see from their faces that it was no story. Jill, belligerent now, said, 'I'm going to come clean because it wasn't my fault and I can't escape. It wasn't anything to do with me. It was the others. They dared her to go to this Orr chap (don't kick me, Penny!) and ask him to sell her this hairdressers.'

'Orr. Gilbert Orr?' Belinda said, on a low horrified note.

They both nodded vigorously, then Jill, evidently thinking better of her attempt to come clean, said, 'He wasn't cross. He just laughed. He took her to tea, and then he sent her back. It was all right. Honestly!'

'Like it was all right sending a note to someone which was supposed to come from me, asking him to come on a journey and give me advice?' Belinda thrust, but at the last moment decided to mention no names. She was glad she hadn't mentioned Derek, because clearly she had drawn a blank here. Neither of these girls knew a thing about that note to Derek signed 'Lulie'. Then who *had* written it?

She got up. 'When are you leaving, Penny? Or isn't that true, either?'

'Tomorrow. The powers-that-be, say I can, because Daddy phoned about me. He was told,' she swallowed, determined now to tell Belinda everything, 'that no one will break their hearts over losing my services. I've been recommended to think of some way of being of use to people.'

Belinda had an insane desire to laugh, because Penny, while not actually mimicking anyone, had certainly quoted someone they all knew very well. That dry comment was just like her! 'Well, don't forget anything when you pack, and don't worry Mummy and Daddy when you get home. Oh, and don't tell anyone else about this, either of you. No one *does* know about it, do they?' she asked, as an appalled afterthought, and apparently the whole of their set knew.

Penny and Jill suddenly had a need to be elsewhere and bolted to the door. Belinda, momentarily defeated, followed them, wondering how it was all going to end.

As she went back to her own room, she wondered if she'd confide in Zoë. It was an appealing idea. She badly wanted to talk things over with someone. But Zoë was out. She remembered it as she looked into her friend's empty room. Dr Elliott would still be out, too. She had to think, so she put on her coat and went for a walk. It was a starlit night, cold, bright, dry. She stood at the gate of the Nurses' Home, drinking in the crisp air. She still had an hour before she need be in. Her father always begged her not to walk about the streets of Spanwell alone and because she knew it worried him she usually managed to go out with either Zoë or a group of other nurses, or a man friend. But tonight there was so much on her mind, she forgot, and walked briskly down the street, into the slightly darker street at the end. Spanwell was made up of a network of small streets lying behind the major roads, the well-lit shopping thoroughfares. A nurses uniform was usually a safeguard, too, in this district, but she still had on her mufti, her dark hair piled high and glinting ear-studs in her ears. Not much of the nurse about her tonight, and she was looking at the ground thinking as her high-heeled court shoes tapped along. It was a real shock to her when a dark shadow reared itself from a darkened doorway and a tall young man stood in front of her, blocking her path. She gasped, then she saw it was the good-looking man in the photo.

'Oh, it's you!' she said. 'Well, I just happened to want to speak to you. How was it that Fergus Jopling knew who you were and I didn't?'

His jaw dropped, but he quickly recovered himself. 'That's easily remedied, love. You can get to know me right now. How about a little walk in a quieter neighbourhood?'

She shook his hand off her arm. 'Don't be an idiot. I'm in the vicinity of my hospital, and it's on behalf of the patient that I want to know your name!'

He laughed and drew her along. He might look a light-weight young man who lounged about, but his grip on her arm was of steel.

She struggled, angrily, but that merely amused him. 'Oh, you want to play hard to get?' and he moved suddenly and she was crushed against him, all her struggles for nothing.

A dark shadow was purring along by them and stopped, and a man got out of a car, his voice like the lash of a whip. 'How much longer am I supposed to wait, Belinda, and what sort of friends do you keep on the side?'

She didn't recognise the voice, but it had the ring of authority, and the good-looking man from the photo Jill had procured, let go of Belinda at once and hurried off into the shadowed end of the street without another word.

'Many thanks, whoever you are!' Belinda said quickly. 'I don't know how you know my name, but I don't seem to know you. Have you been a patient in our hospital or a visitor–?'

'Good heavens, don't you remember my voice? I'm Orr. You've not long ago given me six of the (verbal) best on the telephone, about your young sister.'

'Oh.' Belinda's tones descended to freezing point. 'Then I'm glad I met you. I want to tell you–'

'Let me tell you something first,' he cut in. 'I was sitting out there in my car, after using a nearby callbox. I wanted to see if she'd come whooping out to get a cab to go to my place, as she usually does. (Oh, yes, didn't you know?) And if she had done that, I was going straight inside that hospital to speak to someone in authority about her. It was amusing at first, but it got too much of a good thing. I would have felt better, I admit, if I'd known she had an older sister like you, in the background.'

'Why did you let her contact you at all, after the first time?' Belinda fumed.

'Can you stop her doing things? I thought not. Your face is a dead giveaway, and I bet you have enough on your plate through the similarity in voices, now confess it! It's rather uncanny, actually.'

'Yes, well, I'm glad you are not going to see my sister again, Mr Orr. And thank you for intervening just now. I must go. Goodnight.'

He said a civil goodnight and made no attempt to stop her. But as she didn't return to the hospital but walked along the dark end of the street, he drove his car along until he reached her. 'Going to court more trouble? That young devil may be waiting around. If you want to get away from the hospital for a bit, come in my car. (Oh, be your age, I won't hurt you. Not interested.) But I would like to ask a few things about that young sister of yours.'

Belinda was torn between such a fool-hardy thing as going in a stranger's car after what had been happening to Penny, and her desire and need to know more.

He laughed at her hesitation. 'Hardly polite to me, having rescued you from a fate worse than death, is it? Well, all right, just sit in my car, with the door open so you can fall out to safety if I attack you. But at least take the weight off your feet and tell me a few things I want to know about that sister of yours. Poison with the face of an angel, that girl. And it's no use looking like that at me – I imagine you feel somewhat murderous towards her yourself at times!' He patted the seat. 'Come on, chance it. You're within screaming distance of the hospital, but if you'd like me to drive up to the gates and park there in full view of the nursing staff–?'

She said, 'Oh, no. Sorry, but I'm so worried about Penny, I hardly know what I'm doing.' She sat beside him, but she did leave the door open, rather to his sardonic amusement. 'When did you first get to know my sister?'

He told her, briefly. She thought with a shock – that would be the time her sister had told the patient about it. She said, 'You've only known her a couple of weeks then,' and she sounded relieved.

'Wrong,' he said. 'I've known her for some months.' He listened in acute interest to Belinda's gasp of dismay. 'Is it possible you didn't know anything about this?' But he could see she didn't.

He reached up and put on the light. He

137

wanted to watch her face. Belinda said, 'Tell me about the first time you met her. I need to know. She's pestering my parents to have her home. She doesn't want to nurse any more.'

'Oh, so that's how she got out of it,' he said obscurely. When Belinda wanted to know what that meant, he was silent, then shrugged. 'She really should have got into deep trouble. It would have taught her a lesson. As it is, she's being baled out again. She came to my flat. Alone.' He watched Belinda closely, and added, 'At night. In mufti. Make-up skilfully put on. Impossible to tell she was only eighteen. Not that it would have mattered. They tell me I'm a cad.'

Belinda sat watching him, her heart beating uncomfortably fast. He didn't know it but she was suddenly remembering rumours that were going the rounds, that one of the young nurses was perpetually staying out late but that she had friends who let her in in a variety of ways. But one day authority would be tipped off and the girl would be caught. Belinda, bothered by so many things, had never thought for a moment that that girl could be Penny. But now she was hearing Adam Elliott's voice in her head, repeating that remark of his, that Penny sat apparently in rapt attention looking at him in his lectures, but he could see she wasn't really there. She was away in some world of her own, yet as she was looking at him, apparently listening, he could do nothing about it.

'Your sister amused me that first time, with her outrageous proposition. She said she was so rich, she really didn't know why she wanted to buy the property with the hairdressers in it, but she did, and there it was.'

'She doesn't look like a rich girl,' Belinda said bitterly.

'Oddly enough, she did. She was dressed plainly, but the way she carried it off, suggested careless wealth. I know. And that girl knows. Why the heck don't you all let her be an actress? She'd be good at that. Dash it, her whole life is an act in a play. Especially on my yacht.'

Belinda merely gasped. It was all getting so outrageous that she began to feel that this man was the actor, spinning an improbable story for some reason known to himself ... except that Penny had told part of this story to the patient.

'I took her aboard with some other people. There was a party. Everyone was drinking, but she didn't. I've discovered since that she doesn't like the stuff, and what she doesn't like, she doesn't have. She doesn't like petting parties, either. I know – I tried. Don't waste your breath upbraiding me, love. Like I told you on the phone, I'm no boy. I'm a grown man and I take my pleasures as they come. But your sister's a hard-headed little

139

brat who thinks about only one thing … Penny herself. You just remember that! She never mentioned you. She said her parents were rich and bored and out of the country, leaving her to get on as best she could. Spare your fury it won't help! Penny's Penny – fun while it lasts.'

'You're the most hateful man I ever met,' Belinda murmured.

'I can't dispute that. What's your father, by the way? Really an industrialist?'

'No. Local G.P. And my mother was a nurse. And they did so want us both to be in nursing.'

'And you stuck it out, to please them?'

'No. I wanted to be a nurse. I love my work. Please don't comment on that, either. It means too much to me to have cheap jokes about it.'

He leaned back and took his hat off, slinging it on the back seat. She watched him uneasily, but there were still things she had to know. He had a thin face, a hard mouth; it was the face of a man who had kicked his way up the ladder, made great wealth and wasn't going to lose it quickly or foolishly. A man who had had to find his own pleasures and pay for them, so he was discriminating. Greed had no part of his nature; probably because he knew what happened to the greedy ones. Caution and cold common sense were his attributes, and he was as interested in women as he would be in property and possessions: coldly, distantly.

'I wasn't going to make cheap jokes about it,' he told her. 'I wouldn't like them to be made about my all-consuming passion – that of being a property developer. And you still want to know things about your sister, don't you? Sure? Sure you won't be sickened?'

'We were a happy family once. I suppose the baby of the family can be spoilt in more ways than one. She's been spoilt all right. What else *could* she have done, though, than take on dares from the rest of her idiot set?'

'She pestered me, because she didn't like being treated as the kid she was. She wanted to come out to Brotton Manor. You don't know it? It's a crumbling old Tudor place, just outside Brottonfold. I bought it for myself. Oh, not to live in. A smart flat, service type, is all I need. No, I thought I'd stop the crumbling, and turn it into a country club. She wanted to see it. I said she wasn't to go there, but it's no use telling Penny no. Two idiot boys, friends of hers, drove her out there and the story was she got herself locked in.'

'Oh, I don't believe it!' Belinda exploded. 'Now really, you are going too far. She always goes out with two boys and a girl-friend – a foursome. And she's always in in time. There would have been an unholy row if she hadn't been.'

'You *are* living in a fool's paradise! Don't

141

you know anything that goes on?'

'I've been on night duty,' she admitted, rather breathlessly. Could it be true she asked herself. Could it? Must be something bad for Penny to drive their father into ringing up the hospital to secure her release. But would someone else get into trouble in Penny's place? 'Your sister was there till after one thirty in the morning. She knew I was going there. Later I decided not to. I was going off the place a bit. Then I got a bit nagged when she didn't show up at my flat by ten thirty, which she usually did without warning. I telephoned the hospital and her friend got in a panic and said they'd taken her out to the manor and left her there. Yes, you may well sit up! I got skids under my heels. I drove like a maniac out to Brotton to rescue her but she wasn't there. It seems that her friend got panicky and telephoned to the two boys. Got them out of bed to go and get Penny. They got her in somehow. I don't know what happened.'

A car drove through, slowed down as if the people were looking to see what was wrong with Gilbert Orr's car. He shrugged, put out the light and told Belinda to close her door. He started the car up and drove out of the street, round the block and pulled up outside the Nurses' Home. 'I think I'll collect you tomorrow to tell you the next thrilling story about your sister. What time?'

'No, Mr Orr,' Belinda said, nearer to tears than she had thought possible. 'I may well be in dire trouble myself by then. I think that was one of the doctors in that car. I shall have some explaining to do. And as my sister is going home anyway, it really can't matter what else she has done, so long as it doesn't get around.' She looked at him. Her young face was taut with anxiety and appeal. He frowned. Now really, he told himself, having got rid of the younger Fenn girl, he simply mustn't get interested in the older one. 'Point taken,' he said curtly.

EIGHT

When Belinda telephoned home her father confirmed that Penny had been getting so upset that they had said she could go home. 'Giving up nursing isn't such a bad thing if you just don't like it,' her father said, as if he were trying to convince himself. 'Anyway, the hospital seemed to think it a good idea.'

'What will Penny do to keep herself occupied?' Belinda asked blankly.

'Her mother wants to go away and recuperate so I said Penny should go with her. Oh, it won't be expensive. I've a patient with relatives living down on the south coast. It will be good for recuperation, and,' he sighed, 'the house will be quiet, just myself here alone.'

Well, nothing much could go wrong with Penny away at the sea with her mother, Belinda supposed. Her father said suddenly, 'And you, Bel – what about you; are you – have you anything to tell me?'

'I don't suppose I have. Penny will have told you about the patient, I suppose.'

'Then it's true.' He sounded as if he didn't want to believe it. 'I thought you wanted to make your career in hospital, Bel!'

'I did,' she said, striving to sound casual, and not blaming Penny. 'Actually one of the doctors thinks I need not stick to that promise. He thinks I'd do better staying on finishing my nursing in hospital.'

'If you've made a promise like that, Bel, you must stick to it,' her father said, with unexpected finality.

When she had replaced the receiver, she stared out into the brightness of the grounds. It was the following day. Penny had got transport home – she would! Unwin Calder, Bel supposed. Meantime Bel had a few days off, and she didn't know what to do with them. Not so long ago there would have been a hundred things to do. She was glad, in a way, when the patient sent for her to see him.

He was better and sitting up, she saw, and the ward sister told her that it would do him a power of good, would put his mind at rest about things he wanted to talk to her about, but that she shouldn't stay longer than half an hour.

Left alone, Belinda took a deep breath and went in, but got a shock to see her young sister standing by Fergus Jopling's bed.

Penny said quickly, before she could speak, 'It's all right! He *knows!* He guessed it ages ago! Didn't you?' she appealed to him. 'Anyway, I only came in to say goodbye. My friends are going to drive me home. Did you know I was to go away with Mummy to recuperate, Bel?' And with a bright wave of the hand to the patient as she went, she almost skipped out of the ward.

'I didn't know,' Belinda said weakly.

'Sit down,' Fergus Jopling said, so she pulled out the stool from under the bed, and sat by him. '*Your* hand that was always holding mine?' he queried, taking hers, then closing his eyes, considered the hand in his. 'Yes, *your* hand. Steady, cool, the hand that gave me confidence. Why didn't you give me credit for guessing and not treat me like a fool?'

'I was under orders,' she told him quietly. 'We weren't to know you'd guess. You were often under sedation. Time has little meaning, nor people, in those circumstances.'

'Well, so now we have solved the mystery, who made the promise, which I fully intend to hold someone to.'

'You must know that my sister is not yet nineteen – only just starting to be a student nurse. Anyway, she must have told you she's leaving the hospital.'

'Because of this matter?'

'No, because of a hundred other matters, which really don't come into this. I am the only qualified nurse, and the promise was made in my name, I understand.'

'If I'd asked you to make the promise, what would have been your answer?'

'I can't say, Mr Jopling. I don't know just how upset a refusal would have made you,' Belinda said.

'Well, that's honest. And now we know the truth, will you come and talk to me sometimes? Oh, I suppose all those entertaining stories came from the other one,' and he smiled, a small tight smile of unwilling amusement. Belinda nodded. 'They were just stories. No truth in them?' he asked suddenly.

'Would it matter?' Belinda asked, carefully.

'Yes, if it meant that she would be a source of trouble and anxiety to you in the future, so that it took your mind off my nephew.' And there the matter rested, for the time being, for Sister looked in and signalled for Belinda to leave. Fergus Jopling protested he still had important things to say, but they were smilingly swept aside till next time.

'He looks better,' she told Belinda outside. 'You're good for people!'

Belinda couldn't agree with that, especially when she found Dr Elliott just outside, talking to Hope Kingston, who was half in and half out of her new car, a gleaming expensive toy which must have cost a great deal. Belinda was frowning: she had just remembered that she hadn't asked the patient about the photo, though that perhaps was just as well. Nothing controversial in discussion just yet!

Controversial discussions were the order of the day for Belinda herself, however. Hope Kingston broke off speaking to Dr Elliott, looked at the approaching Belinda, and raised her eyebrows, so that he looked round. They must have been speaking about her, Belinda thought, for Dr Elliott left Hope, almost as if by pre-arrangement. Hope got into her car but sat there watching, a bright interested smile on her hard young face. Dr Elliott waited for Belinda to come up to where they stood.

He said, 'Was it you, Nurse, in that car with its light on, in the street behind the hospital last night?'

Belinda was furious. Did he have to ask the question in Hope's hearing? It didn't concern her! So she said sweetly, 'What car, Dr Elliott?' and as she kept walking, he fell in beside her.

'That wasn't very polite, to walk away from Miss Kingston's car. She was in the conversation. It was she who pointed you out to me!'

'But she's already told you that I am friends with the new Casualty Officer. Does she mean to alter that story and make it that I'm friends with someone else?'

He reddened. 'She means well. She knows the chap who was in the car with you. She says he's a dreadful bounder.'

'And she may well be right, for all I know, but since I don't know who she's talking about, and since my friends are no business of Sir Maxwell's niece, I do really think you should go back to Miss Kingston, Dr Elliott, and not bother about me.'

'Oh, don't be ridiculous, Bel. You must know very well why I worry about you!' he snapped, and then his eyebrows went up comically. 'Sorry, didn't mean to shout at you, but you do really annoy me at times, you know.'

'Then don't speak to me. There's no need. My young sister has left the hospital today, and I shall be leaving it very soon. I am taking up the promise I had made for me to the patient, Fergus Jopling,' she said, making up her mind on the instant.

There really was no need for him to look so aghast, she thought, in swift puzzlement. She was really nothing to him; everyone agreed that he and Hope Kingston were about to become engaged even if it wasn't settled yet, and certainly Hope behaved in such a casual familiar manner as to make one think, Bel thought, that she was his wife already. So why should he look so aghast at the thought of Bel's having promised to take on a private nursing case for someone, for perhaps years to come? A good many nurses might like such a permanent job. It wasn't as if she wanted to marry anyone. Now, she thought, her heart lurching – if she had had the chance to become the wife of a doctor, such as Dr Elliott, for instance... She caught herself up swiftly, appalled at such an idea. He wasn't free, he never had been free, apparently, for her or anyone else to entertain such an idea.

Adam Elliott said, 'Have you thought about it? Are you really sure, Bel?'

She shrugged. 'Everyone else seems to agree with me, and to think I should keep that promise. You, too!'

'Yes, but I've gone into it more deeply since I–' he began, but broke off as Hope blared with determination on her car horn. Impatiently, he said, 'Oh, I'll just go back and tell her– Wait for me!'

Belinda had no intention of waiting for him. What sort of game did he think he was playing? How funny, a man like Derek knew Bel despised him for trying to keep two girls on the hook at the same time – herself and

Marcia. But to think that Adam Elliott was the same! It didn't bear thinking about. Men! She told herself she was better without them and went back to the Nurses' Home.

Now she had three blank days before her. Not so long ago she would not have had any bewilderment as to how to spend them. She had been looking forward to time off; time in which to pull up on rest, sleep, doing a few shopping trips she wanted, and certainly going home. Now there was no need to go home, and perhaps better not – Penny would be getting ready to take her mother off to the home of her father's patient's relations by the sea, and the house would be in total uproar. Besides, how could she hope to keep off this subject, if she were at home at the same time as Penny? Especially as her father seemed to think she was hard on Penny already.

She couldn't spend time with Zoë as their duties had been changed. She had hoped Zoë would be off duty at the same time as herself, but in any case Zoë would want to spend what time she had at her disposal with her boy-friend. Little by little those two seemed to have drawn together closer, while Belinda had been in the middle of this queer business. And now she was out of it and at a loss to know what to do.

She didn't have long to be in that state. Derek telephoned her, saying he was off duty and wanted to see her and could he take her to lunch? She couldn't think of any reasonable excuse for not going, especially as he said bitterly, 'It's all over the hospital that you're now going out with this chap in the huge black car. You're getting yourself talked about, Lulie!'

'Please Derek, for the last time, stop calling me that! It's all over! I told you so! And besides, I thought you were in a terrible state about Marcia?'

'That girl makes a fool of me every so often to suit herself,' he said bitterly. 'How would you feel if you thought someone was in trouble and stuck your neck out and then got a note saying she was all right but had a new bloke?'

'Oh, she's all right, then! Well, I'm glad of that! What with that note you said I'd written, and the fact that you thought she was missing and in danger–'

'Who mentioned danger?' he asked quickly.

'Well, perhaps you didn't, but I got the feeling you meant that. And besides, we haven't cleared up who wrote that note that was supposed to have come from me.'

'Oh, that,' he said. 'I know who wrote it. No, I won't tell you over the telephone. Come to lunch with me, if you want to know.'

And of course, she did. So much that she didn't query his invitation any more, but arranged to go out and meet him.

He looked thinner, she thought, as she got

into his car at the end of the road behind the hospital. 'Are you not happy in your new job, Derek?' she asked. It was just a kindly question, the sort Belinda would have asked any colleague, but he looked absurdly pleased.

'Oh, good, I thought you didn't care any more. No, I'm not happy. It's not the same and I shall leave just as soon as my year is up. I don't know why I wanted to come back here except–'

'Except what?' she asked idly.

'You must know,' he said, looking oddly embarrassed. 'Oh, I know Marcia is ... well, Marcia. She can twist me round her little finger and make me feel a king but when the chips are down, it's you. You're the person a chap wants to lean on, to be sure of. Well, you know that. You must do! No use shaking your head and saying it's all over. I don't want it to be. Please, Lulie (Oh, hell, I can't stop using that little name!) please let it be *on* again.'

She shook her head at him. 'I suppose, harsh though it may sound, I've grown out of the things I used to do, the people I used to like. I seem to have got very much older these last few weeks even. It's the worry of Penny, I suppose.'

'Oh, and the patient that was being specialled,' he said knowledgeably. 'Well, I know it was supposed to be kept dark, but you know the way Penny and her bunch go around talking at the top of their voices. I don't suppose many people haven't heard something or other she's been talking about at some time.'

'I didn't know you knew my sister!' she said blankly, but he merely shrugged. 'I made it my business to find out about her, since you seemed so worried about her and the minute I saw her, I knew what sort of burden she could be to you.'

In Adam Elliott, that sentiment could have been entirely different. In Derek, she resented it and said fiercely, 'She isn't a burden. And anyway, she's left the hospital now, so nobody need think about her any more. She didn't like nursing.' She took a hold of herself, tamped down her anger. 'Anyway, I didn't come here to talk about Penny. I came to find out who had written that note, copying my handwriting. The person must be stopped, before she does any more damage.'

'Then you don't think it was your sister?'

'Derek, I am keeping my patience. Never mind what I think. You said you *know* who it was, so please tell me. Now! It's all I agreed to lunch with you for.'

'Well, thanks very much. What's happened to my boyish charm?' he retorted. 'As to who it is, in this mood, you'll create such a furore, I really think I'd be a lunatic to tell you at this moment. No, I'll tell you later, when it's all died down but I can assure you, it won't happen again because I also happen to know why the person did it.'

'But you must tell me, if you know! It's a terrible thing for someone to have done!' she said angrily, and noticed how distressed he looked. 'I suppose it was Marcia, for mischief, after all,' she added, and he didn't trouble to deny it.

It turned out to be a very exhausting and packed day. Belinda got away from Derek as soon as she could, and while he drove back to the hospital, she stayed for an afternoon's shopping. Spanwell's big shops were adequate, and somehow she had let her wardrobe run down. She had promised herself for some time that she would get a new dress for the social occasions that the hospital reluctantly provided every month. Other nurses of her year kept four such dresses rotating so that they didn't get dated, but Belinda was lazy about shopping, and since Derek's time, there had been no other special boy-friend, there had hardly seemed to be any need. Now, faced with the one dress everyone must know by now, she decided it would be a tonic to buy a new one.

But the shopping expedition was spoilt by running into Hope Kingston coming out of the next department, carrying a dress-box in her hands, and talking angrily to a young man who vaguely reminded Belinda of Dr Elliott.

Belinda was behind a stand, and heard Hope say, 'Please, Oswald, for pity's sake don't be such a *bore!* You're hard up – I'm hard up – and no, I can't manage to squeeze any more out of Uncle. He's such a tight-wad lately, I can't think why.'

The young man tightened his weak mouth into lines of obstinacy. 'What's wrong with asking your mother then?' but Hope stared at him with distaste. 'Do you really think I'd go *there*, and ask *her* for money? Don't be an idiot, I'd have an inquisition, anyway, as to why I wasn't pushing on with my engagement to your dear cousin Adam. Honestly, it's the one thing in the world she can talk about! I even get it on the telephone now!'

'Well, I thought that's what you wanted,' the young man said, trying to prise Hope from a stand of silk scarves she was paying more attention to now.

'It's what I'm going to *get*,' Hope said, between her teeth. 'And as he never seems short of cash, it will be the one consolation. So leave me alone!'

Belinda prayed Hope would move on. She was caught in this little alley of dress stands. It was a dead end, no way out. Oswald said, 'Well, if you won't ask your mother for money, I shall have to ask my revered cousin, and that will get me nowhere fast. So ... it will have to be another cheque.'

Hope was horrified. 'No! No, don't involve

Lloyd again,' she begged. Belinda was shocked to hear such a change in that girl's usually cold, malicious, or over-bearing tones. Whatever else Hope had been, it was never fearful, as her voice was now. 'I'll get you some money, believe me I will, but for heaven's sake make it last. Only don't use Lloyd's name any more, *please.*'

Belinda almost didn't hear the last of that, it was so quietly spoken. The silence blanketed the place. New people came and talked about measurements. Belinda realised Hope and Oswald had gone, and she could reasonably come out.

She felt appalled at having been an unwilling witness to that curious conversation – a conversation desperate enough to be softly carried out behind dress racks – and now she realised who Oswald was. This must be the cousin Adam had spoken about, the one who had been brought up as a brother. How could Adam Elliott have a cousin like that? And did he know his cousin was on such terms with Hope? Belinda doubted it.

Now she wanted to get out of the place. She saw a bus just about to pull out, heading for Cheppingstock. There were nice places between Spanwell and there. She didn't want to go right into Cheppingstock because of the memories lingering from the time Adam took her there to dinner, a dinner that had been ruined by Hope and her brother. So she got off a few miles before Cheppingstock, and began to walk briskly down a side road signposted to Brottonfold. That was where the old property was, she recalled, that belonged to Gilbert Orr, the place where Penny had gone late at night, and caused such consternation among her friends.

Curious to see the place, Belinda walked briskly on. Her thoughts ranged over all the strange things that had been happening to her since she had started to 'special' Fergus Jopling, and to speculate what her future would be, now she had committed herself to take over Penny's disastrous promise. What sort of a man was Fergus Jopling, to hold a nurse to such a promise which had been made by an irresponsible young sister?

It wasn't entirely a surprise to be passed by Gilbert Orr in that big car of his. He had been out to look at his property, she thought, angry at being caught so near it. She didn't want that man to think she was interested.

He stopped, and backed along. 'Hello, where are you off to, Nurse?' he asked.

Useless to pretend she didn't know Brotton was near.

'Well, anywhere within the time at my disposal,' she said carelessly. 'As my sister had expressed such an odd interest in Brotton Manor, I decided it might be a good terminus for a walk, if I can get a bus back. That's all.'

'Well, you won't. I suppose you got the Cheppingstock bus. The return one doesn't come this way. Want to compromise yourself by letting me drive you?'

He always made her feel such a fool, with that sardonic smile of his. She supposed Penny was so full of her pretty young self that it never occurred to her that this man could be quietly laughing at her, but Belinda was very much aware of his sly amusement at her expense, so she said, 'I'll take a chance. I can't do much else without transport, can I?'

'Ungracious,' he commented. 'Why do you hate me so much?'

She didn't trouble to deny that she didn't like him though she was moved to point out that hatred was too strong a word. 'And as you're giving me transport, perhaps you'd do what you said you would, and fill in the rest of the story about my young sister.'

'What time do you have to be back at the hospital? You're off nights now, I know that; don't tell me you just have half an hour, because I've telephoned the hospital to find out. I was coming to pick you up actually.'

'Why?' she asked in surprise.

'I don't know, really. Nothing on my hands at this moment. No need to worry about your sister as she appears to have really gone home. And you are the only sane woman I happen to know, and I want an honest opinion about Brotton Manor.'

'I can't give you an opinion about a property. That's your job!'

'You could give an opinion about anything, if you wanted to. By instinct.'

She coloured in annoyance. It was true, she often had an instinctive feeling that proved right, without specialised knowledge. But she didn't like this man to be so shrewd. But at that point, the road ahead cleared, as if a giant hand stretched down each side and parted the overhanging trees, so that the view ahead was all light; a good clear view across a shallow valley, and deep in it nestled a house. All humped red roof, lichen covered, with twisty Elizabethan chimneys, tangled creeper making havoc of guttering, the walls stained with age, the colour washed out of dark cross beams by a multiple number of winter storms. Utterly beautiful and picturesque as a postcard scene, but unpractical for someone like Gilbert Orr to dabble with.

He didn't have to ask her. By the time he had driven them down, through the tipsy wrought iron gates perpetually open because of the long grass that had taken over the drive, he could see all he wanted to in her face. 'I expect tramps have made a home in there,' Belinda murmured, regretfully. 'How come it was ever allowed to decay like that?'

'Decay. You've said it, lass. I suppose nobody wanted it. I didn't buy it. Not as a straight sale, that is. I gave a knock-down price for that, the land, and several other properties, to the Executors, to wind up the Estate. I can't grumble. The other properties were little town houses. I've made a profit on them. But this … it did seem a good idea, if only because of the locale, to turn it into a kind of country club. No?'

'Don't be guided by me. I would have thought you'd know yourself, with your special knowledge, what you could or couldn't do with an old place.'

He stopped the car, some way away from the crumbling front steps. 'I suppose every so often I come over romantic,' he complained, which made her laugh. 'No? You don't think so? You'd be surprised. Want to go inside and look?'

'Well, I'd like to see the main hall, but I don't suppose I shall want to go much further, from the look of the outside,' she said. 'Where did my sister Penny go, in the dark, in this place?'

He was amused, wryly amused. 'I have since heard she didn't go inside. Not because she was particularly scared – I don't believe that kid scares easily. No, it struck her that it would soil her new dress so she stayed outside. Besides, she complained of hearing noises. I had warned her it was a tramp's paradise so what did she expect?'

'Can't you keep it boarded up to keep them out?' Belinda asked idly. She was in no way repelled by tramps. Too often in the past, it had been her unenviable job to clean up a tramp and have him admitted, while on Casualty stint. Tramps got skin diseases through eating mouldy bread, and rheumatism was not unknown to them, spending such a lot of their lives in damp shelters or out all night in the rain. But she didn't say so. This man would be filled with distaste at what a nurse would be required to do, she was sure.

'How could I do that effectively?' he asked idly, as he helped her out of the car. He threw a large stone at part of the brickwork, and it crumbled, and slowly fell out. 'It was built in an era when building was good, but bricks don't last for ever, especially with neglect.'

'What a shame,' she said, and let him take her arm to go up the front steps and through a door that looked as if it must, when new, have been built so sturdy to keep out invaders. The great iron studs had wept rust down the woodwork, staining it in sad red trickles, but the door was still good and strong. But somewhere a window clanged miserably on broken hinges, indicating how the tramps got in without effort. From somewhere above, a dismal knocking sounded.

He grinned. 'We won't go up. They're probably pulling down a few shelves for firewood.' He shrugged at her indignation. 'I take it you are not in favour of letting the place go to seed, then? You think I should

161

eject the tenants and do something about costly restoration?'

'Goodness, no, it's none of my business!' she exclaimed, looking round the enormous hall. 'It's just that...' She shivered. 'I feel rather idiotically that the ghosts of former occupants are not very pleased with you for not making a push to keep the place ... in respect...' She broke off, confused.

'You do like it,' he marvelled. 'I thought you would. Damned if I won't get a contractor over to tell me the worst. Well, I can find out what it would cost to put it right.'

'Don't do it for me,' Bel said hastily.

'Well, I wouldn't, would I?' he said, gently mocking. 'Just for me, though. Do it up and sell it, at a profit.'

Trying to ignore the festoons of cobwebs, she looked at the grand staircase, with its five landings, and its carved beasts; the delicate vaulted ceiling and the (now broken) stained glass windows. Birds flew in and out, their droppings on the fine old wood, but it didn't seem to matter because rain kept the woodwork in a dangerous state of damp. Gilbert Orr looked glumly at it, but there was a light of battle in his eyes, or if not battle, perhaps sudden interest, enthusiasm. Belinda was afraid that it was because of what she said, and she drew a deep breath to qualify her remarks, dampen his enthusiasm, when the far-off knocking sound terminated in a cry of pain.

Belinda began to run upstairs. Gilbert Orr, behind her, caught her and held on to her, pulling her back. The tread of the stair she had been about to throw her weight on to, gave way, gently crumbling and falling through beneath. 'Can't you see it's dangerous, damn you?' he muttered, still holding on to her. 'I told you – it's tramps. Probably fighting up there. Let them kill each other.'

Belinda struggled and he reluctantly freed her. 'Don't you know a cry of pain when you hear it? I must go. Help me round the weak spots of the stairs, or is there another way up? How did *they* get up there?'

He spent valuable minutes trying to dissuade her, and played with the idea of forcibly carrying her out, but he could see it was no use. 'Forward the dedicated nurse!' he jeered, but she only said, 'Of course!' in a preoccupied way, and carefully found a way up at the side of the rotting staircase. Gilbert glumly followed her. 'There's no need for you to come,' she said. 'Much better if you went to a telephone and called an ambulance, as soon as I find out what's wrong. I'll call down to you!'

'All right,' he surprised her by saying. 'It won't hold the weight of both of us. If you're so stuck on messing about with tramps, go and see what the damage is and let me know,' and he brushed down his impeccable suit.

She directed a look of scorn down on him and hurried upstairs. And so he didn't know what happened in the attics when Belinda discovered – not tramps, but a man bending threateningly over a bundle which turned out to be a girl with red hair. Belinda stood stock still in the doorway of the vast attic space, and stared open-mouthed at the man for an instant. 'You!' Gilbert Orr heard her say, but he didn't hear her mutter, 'And Marcia. Is she ... is she all right?' Nor did he hear the mocking male voice say, 'Naturally. I have too much sense to kill her, though she asks for it!'

'Wait there. I'll get an ambulance,' Belinda said, eyeing the wound on the girl's head with doubt. 'Don't touch her. I don't know what you've done.'

'I didn't hit her. She fell,' was the cool reply.

Belinda rushed down to the broken staircase where Gilbert Orr waited. 'It's a girl I know. She's got a head wound. Would you drive to the nearest telephone – I want an ambulance quickly!' and she omitted to mention that two people were up there. So Gilbert Orr hurried to do as she asked, and in no time at all, it seemed the ambulance from Spanwell arrived. But by that time Marcia was alone. A flapping door at the end of the attic, to another staircase down to the lower regions was all there was to indicate that Marcia hadn't been alone. And much later, when she came to she steadily said that she had had nobody with her. It was Belinda's word against hers.

NINE

Adam faced Belinda as she came down from Marcia's ward. The girl was still unconscious, and Belinda was oddly worried about her condition. It hadn't seemed such a bad head wound that she had looked at, but on admission, it appeared that there was another wound. Now Marcia was gravely ill. Belinda, remembering Derek's shocked face as he had admitted her through Casualty, wondered why he had had to be on duty at that time. But she was preoccupied with the thought that it had not been grief so much as fear in his face. Fear? Derek? The two things didn't seem to tie up at all.

She looked dazedly at Adam, who repeated his question. 'Bel, how came you to be at that old ruin of a house with a chap like Orr? How did you come to know him?'

'What's wrong with him?' she asked, not understanding the drift of his words.

He took her arm and led her into an embrasure that looked down on the back of the yard where the ambulances were.

165

Neither of them saw any details of the busy scene below, nor the Spanwell streets beyond them. Adam said, 'Bel, I don't know what's happening. I have been trying so hard to get you to myself for a quiet talk but we get so many interruptions. I believe you're anxious, that you have trouble even, and I want to help you. Why won't you trust me?'

'I'd like to,' she admitted blankly, 'but people keep warning me that Miss Kingston won't like it and anyway–'

He frowned. 'I don't see how it concerns Hope, what you and I discuss, and certainly she wouldn't be interested. Why were you at Brotton Manor?'

She looked at her hands. She would have loved to tell someone, and as she stood in this embrasure with him, his quiet strength flowed out to her, and tempted her. They were perhaps more private here than if he instigated a trip out in his car, where almost certainly Hope Kingston would appear, though Belinda couldn't think how it happened so often, unless Hope had a lot of time to spare and followed him about to see he didn't take other girls out. And nobody was likely to find him to carry him off to one of the wards, so she made up her mind and began. But her opening sentences showed her how difficult it was going to be.

'You see, as I've made this promise, it will take me to the house where the nephew of

Mr Jopling lives, and as far as I can see, there won't be much time to do any shopping and I haven't many clothes, so I went to a store in town. Well, I have three days off–'

'I know,' he broke in, 'and I got time off too, to be with you, but you made it plain you didn't want my company so I came back on duty. I would have driven you to the shops. It might have been fun,' he said, with an odd little smile, 'to go with you to carry the dress boxes.'

He was talking like a man who was free, and getting tenderly interested in a girl, she thought confusedly. And it wasn't so. She plunged on: 'Well, I was interrupted, by being caught in one of those silly situations where I couldn't get out without letting the people talking realise I'd heard their conversation. So I had to stay. And they were people I knew; I was embarrassed and upset, and I went out as soon as I could and got on a bus.'

'Why?' His uncomplicated mind couldn't accept such a way to behave.

'I just wanted to get out of the town. I was filled with distaste with what I'd heard. I wished I could forget it. Well, I couldn't. So I got off the bus after a while and walked, and when I saw the sign to Brotton Manor I remembered my sister Penny had apparently gone there one night so I was going to walk and see what it looked like. It's a ruin.'

'I know that. How did Orr come into it?'

he asked, anger replacing his former half tender, half smiling mood.

She shrugged. 'He'd been there, and was driving away. He said he'd drive me there and show me the place if I was interested. He wanted an unbiased view on it.'

'He *wha-at?* That chap? How you let people take you in, Bel!'

'Yes, don't I?' she said levelly. 'Apparently my sister Penny hadn't gone inside because it was in a mess and dangerous. The stairs are broken.'

'And as I hear you rescued an injured girl from the attics I suppose you went up those dangerous stairs without thought of your own safety!'

'Dr Elliott, I don't see why you should be angry with me for doing what any nurse would have done in the circumstances.'

'Where was Orr?' he asked angrily, so she answered quietly enough. 'I made him wait so I could call down to him about her injuries and sent him to the nearest tele-phone to call the ambulance.'

'I understand that everyone is of the impression that someone else was there when you found her, but managed to vanish. What was all that about?'

His face held open disbelief. He wanted to believe her but he felt she was hiding things to protect her sister. She could see that. 'I know Penny has left the hospital, but she may come back to this district and I want to find out everything she did, to protect her. I didn't like her being friends with Mr Orr, but he didn't do her any harm, apparently. She bored him. She's too young for him,' she said.

'But *you* are not,' Belinda thought he muttered under his breath.

'Please, Dr Elliott, if you want the full story as I know it, for goodness sake let me rush it out at you before we get interrupted again,' she urged, which was just common sense so he stood silently listening. 'The man who was with Marcia was the man in the first photo that caused Mr Jopling to collapse. Well, he was looking at it when he collapsed and he seemed to know him.'

'Oh, that chap! The one whose name is apparently still a mystery,' he snapped.

'I have no idea. I only know that Marcia had vanished, and that the Casualty Officer merely contacted me to help him find her. She is the one he is keen on,' she said firmly, as Adam's brow darkened. 'And I thought you were going to ask Sir Maxwell about him,' Belinda reminded him.

'I did. Sir Maxwell didn't know what I was talking about. He hadn't seen such a person. Nor did his secretary know of him.'

'But that's not possible! I saw him leave Sir Maxwell's clinic. He got funny with me in the dark that night, and he was the one

169

with Marcia when we found her.'

'Are you saying this villain in the first photo was holding this girl against her will in a ruined house and caused her injury? A man whose photo mysteriously came to be in the place where the patient's nephew's photo should have been – a nebulous character you saw go into Sir Maxwell's room, which neither he nor his secretary knew a thing about?'

'You don't believe me, to say such a thing, a thing that wouldn't have occurred to me!' Belinda breathed, shocked. Where was the kind friend she was relying on? Who was this man lashed by an anger she didn't understand? 'All I know is, he is not a nice man. He tried to be funny with me that night when you saw me in Gilbert Orr's car. If you want to know, I'd been walking – there were none of my friends free to go with me and I needed some fresh air – and Gilbert Orr came along in his car and sent this chap off. Oh, I could have handled him but it was a nuisance. And how are you concerned, Dr Elliott, in what happens to one of the nurses?' she asked noting with interest that his face had gone puce with anger.

'I think you do know the chap's name, or at least where it can be found. If we can't find it, I shall ask Jopling's nephew – he may know. But meantime, I want the rest of this strange story. I can swallow that that feather-brained sister of yours got involved with people but I also know she has a capacity for getting herself out of trouble. And you haven't. So please tell me who was conducting this conversation in the store which upset you to the point of going off on your own again in deserted lanes where you ran into a man who had already attacked you in a street behind your own hospital!'

'I can't tell! It's no use getting furious. I just won't tell you because you know the people, and anyway, you'd never believe what I said about them.'

'Then it will be my unpleasant duty to take you to your senior nursing officer who, if she can't make you talk, will have to go to higher authority.'

'But why? I've told you how I found Marcia today, and there's no harm in that. Why are you getting so out-of-all-proportion angry, Dr Elliott?'

'Don't you think I would be when I see how you fall flat on your face into new trouble, after the mess you got yourself into over taking on your sister's promise? A criminally careless promise that a very sick man fully intended to hold you to!'

'What's so special about promising to do a long period of private nursing?'

He stared at her, nonplussed. Then he said, 'Are you so devious that you must pretend you think that is all there is in it? Or is it your way of telling me you've made your choice and that I am to mind my own business?'

'Dr Elliott! What can you be thinking? I'd never say–' she began.

'Tell me – who were the people you heard talking in the store? What did they say?'

'I have a good mind to tell you, but you won't believe me. If you do, it will give you pain, I am sure. So why are you pressing?' but she could see he was not going to give way. What was causing this disproportionate anger, she didn't know, unless Hope, possessive and frustrated, had said something. In which case, what good would her telling him do? 'I'll tell Sister, not you,' she decided.

He stood back. 'No, that won't do. If it really concerns me, it occurs to me I just might not want anyone else to know. You seem to be involved in such a tangled mess of other people's actions, heaven knows where it will finish. I wouldn't have thought it of you, of all people. Your younger sister, yes, but not you!'

Oddly, that disparaging remark about Penny stung Belinda so that she lost the urge to protect him from the knowledge she had. 'All right,' she said, between her teeth, 'it was Miss Kingston talking to your cousin, Oswald Vaisey! He wanted money fast and she hadn't got any and he said she was to go to her mother and she wouldn't so

172

he threatened to do what he'd done before, something involving a cheque, which she seemed to think would implicate her brother Lloyd and she begged him not to so, he said he wouldn't if she got money for him so she said she'd try. Then they went away. And I can see from your face that you don't believe a word of it, so why keep bothering me to tell you things?'

As he didn't reply, she said, now thoroughly worked up in her anger, 'And what would you say if I told you that the Casualty Officer had received a letter purporting to come from me, in my handwriting, signed by the little name he used to call me, begging him to come and help me – and I, stupid me, had never seen the note before in my life!'

But that, of course, was going too far. She could see he didn't believe that. 'That,' he remarked coldly, 'has the ring of your young sister about it!' which made matters a lot worse.

'Well, I knew no good would come of succumbing to the temptation to confide in you,' Belinda said crushingly. 'What made me think you were likely to be a friend of mine?'

'A friend?' he was stung to retort. 'Never that! Something else, never that!' a remark she didn't stop to consider, because she had just remembered she had more or less made up her mind to visit Mrs Ivory again today. It would be her only chance during these three days off, and after all, what else had she to do? Then she must go down and see poor Derek about Marcia. She turned towards the stairs marked with the name of the terminal ward she wanted.

'Where do you think you're going, Belinda?'

Not 'Bel'; her full name now. But why her name and not 'Nurse' if he were so put out with her? She had to admit she didn't begin to understand him.

'I'm going up to visit Mrs Ivory,' she said tautly.

'I would have thought it would be the patient in C-12 you'd be visiting,' he said unaccountably. And as she looked perfectly blank, he said patiently, 'The nephew of the late Fergus Jopling, with whom you've become so involved!'

But in all that, all that really mattered to her was the word 'late'. 'The "late" Fergus Jopling?' she repeated, and she went sheet white. The death of a patient was no new thing to her, but that this one should come through so much and now have his life so suddenly ended without anyone telling her, was a real shock. She whitened and swayed a little. Dr Elliott realised at once that she didn't know and leapt forward to support her. 'I'm sorry, Bel, love. I'm sorry. I'm torn apart,' she heard him mutter into her hair, where his face pressed the top of her dark head. 'Oh, Bel,' he murmured brokenly, 'why did all this mess have to happen and what's going to happen to us?' she thought confusedly that he said, through the roaring in her ears, and the support of his arms was not the impersonal clasp of any doctor preventing any nurse from reeling from sudden shock.

'When did he?' she murmured a little later, pushing away from Adam Elliott.

'Just after you went out, I suppose,' and he told her the exact time.

'Was that why you were angry with me, because I wasn't here? I mean, did he ask for me?'

'Bel, think! You know what you've promised, or rather your sister promised in your name and you've decided to keep that promise. Well? Can't you see how I feel? I thought that you, too ... well, perhaps I was mistaken. I must have been mistaken, or you'd never be calmly waiting to take up such a future.'

'There you go again! What's wrong with that sort of future? Loads of nurses would jump at the chance, I suppose! Well, it wasn't my plan, but the sky isn't falling in because that's what I have now got to look forward to.'

'I see,' he said, after a long silence. 'I was mistaken. I don't see how I could have been, but apparently I have. I apologise. I won't trouble you any more. Only...' He rubbed the back of his head and glared at the ground, decided to go on with what he had started, but managed to make it sound curt, not kindly. 'Only if you get stuck in one of those messes you're famous for, or your young sister involves you in something else, come to me for help. Promise me that!'

'No,' she said. 'I feel that this is the promise to end all promises,' and as she didn't yet know the full story of what Penny had involved her in, she still didn't understand why Dr Elliott looked so queerly at her as he turned on his heel and strode away.

Only later, much later, that day was she told that the solicitors of the late Fergus Jopling wanted to see her, and then they would require to talk to both her and Clive Gregory together, in his private room.

They were brief and to the point, because like Dr Elliott, they thought she knew the whole plan. At the end of the consultation, when they departed for London and Belinda walked unsteadily back to the Nurses' Home, she wondered how she could have been so naïve as to think that all the fuss the late Fergus Jopling had been making, could have possibly concerned merely the appointment of a private – a permanently private – nurse for his nephew. Or indeed how she could have been so trusting as to believe Penny could have acted in such a guilty way about making a promise about that sort of appointment. She should have asked more questions. At this stage she blamed Sister

Newman for not allowing her tell the patient about the pairing of the two girls, but that was stupid; he had guessed himself, but of course, the admission came at a time when, although Belinda had been then ready, more than ready, to pepper him with questions, she had been called away, for he was still far from well, and not really up to a long visit from anyone.

And now he had slipped away, relinquishing all his earthly worries, having done his best to protect the massive fortune he had built up over a lifetime, by some clever thinking. Even Belinda, in her shattered state, had to admit that it was clever to bind a girl down to a promise to not only act as a permanent private nurse to a young man who would be a most difficult patient, but also to become his wife. A wife who was considered level-headed enough to inherit and administer that fortune.

Belinda telephoned her father. He was out, of course, and she hadn't got the telephone number of the place where Penny was staying with her mother as she recuperated. Zoë was full of the latest news on her boyfriend, who had gone back on his noble attitude about remaining just 'going steady' because getting engaged involved the expense of a ring. They were going to be engaged and Zoë the unflappable was now walking on air and almost but not quite as giddy as Penny.

Suddenly bereft of anyone to talk to about such a private matter, Belinda did a thing she had promised herself she wouldn't any more, and went out alone in the dark streets of Spanwell, to walk and to think. Fergus Jopling had not only left her with a most truculent young man, a crippled young man moreover, on her hands as patient and husband, but he had left her his fortune, so that Clive couldn't have it.

She went over that scene again, with the solicitors and with Clive Gregory. Clive had been so bitter, especially when she asked him if he had known she was to marry him. He said, 'Oh, yes, I knew about it! And so did you, so why make a mystery of it?'

She eyed him, and the lawyers, and decided it would do no good to try and explain the muddle she had been in. It would lead to the photo and her sister's part in it, and hadn't she tried to protect Penny all this time, and her parents, through Penny's mischievous disposition? Most of all, her father mustn't know! She was glad, then, that he had been out of humour with her when she had telephoned, on those other occasions, or there would surely have been recriminations if she had told him more. But she must tell him now, she had thought, as she had sat there facing Clive and his dark sullen young face.

He was two years older than herself, but he looked such a boy; such a truculent, unlovable boy. 'And you played your cards right,' he had thrust at her, suddenly. 'Got round the old man so that you and only you can get your hands on all his money! What about me?'

The solicitors had interposed, then, that his uncle had been of opinion that he would not have been guided by their advice in the handling of the money, and that he had probably thought this nurse would. Clive had sneered and said, 'What you mean is that my uncle knew what I wanted the money for. Well, it won't stop me. I shall keep on searching for the chap who did this to me and I shall hound him until he–'

Belinda had involuntarily stopped that. 'No! Don't talk like that!' she had interposed swiftly. 'Revenge won't do you any good. But one thing I will do that your uncle didn't want; I shall back you up if you are deemed fit enough for more surgery. I've always felt that if a person wanted surgery no relatives should try to dissuade the patient. It's his body, his life, his pain. I'll help you.'

But Clive hadn't wanted that. He had scowled at her. 'When I want your help I'll ask for it,' he had snapped. 'And let's get this marriage over with. I want the money question settled. If we don't marry, it all goes to charity. Oh, yes, my dear uncle knew how

179

to tie things up all right! And don't think you'll have the cash to sling around, dear nurse, because it won't be yours, either.'

'On the contrary,' the lawyers had interposed. 'Miss Fenn knows perfectly well what your uncle wanted done with the money. In his last letter to us he told us that he had discussed his plans extensively with her, down to the last detail and she agreed.'

Belinda had felt her jaw drop. She was aware that Clive Gregory was watching her keenly, though the solicitors, both elderly and trusting their late client implicitly, saw nothing in her face to worry about. They probably thought she was surprised that he had reported the conversation to them in such detail. Belinda's astonishment was of another sort: clearly it was Penny he had unfolded his plans to. Penny must be contacted somehow and made to tell Belinda exactly what had been planned by the late Fergus Jopling. Belinda must know. It was imperative.

But for a sane man, one who could pile up a fortune, she still couldn't think how he could carry on in such a way. It must, as Adam had insisted, have been because he was not his usual bright self, because of the operation and the drugs and sedatives. Such a way to go on, and with so much at stake!

As she walked along, she was aware that footsteps were matching hers. It was with exasperation that she turned round to discover the good-looking young man in the photo, grinning widely at her discomfiture and falling into step beside her.

'How is the carroty headed beauty then?' he asked her.

'She has a name,' Belinda said acidly. 'And would you mind telling me how she got that other wound on her head? She is very ill indeed.'

'She's a girl who won't see reason,' he said coolly. 'A very selfish girl who wants everything her own way. I pushed her, I regret, and she fell, hitting her head. I am truly sorry about that. I would try to visit her but as I am not related, I fear they wouldn't let me in.'

'They would, if I asked them. Why don't you go and see her?'

'Oh, don't be dashed silly! Do you think she'd want to see me?'

'Then what were you doing at the hospital?'

'I happen to be a patient of Sir Maxwell and I hadn't had my card marked for the next appointment, so I went to find out the next time he'd be there,' he said, shrugging. 'And in any case you say my eyes look all right, let me assure you that I may be having an operation on them, soon.'

Belinda nodded, preoccupied. It wasn't true, but she couldn't put a finger on what he was really doing. She thought of the day when he had been in Sir Maxwell's room for no more than a few minutes, and came out tucking notes, treasury notes, into his breast pocket. He hadn't behaved like a patient, and he certainly wouldn't have been allowed to jump the queue of people who were already sitting patiently in rows, waiting for Sir Maxwell's clinic to open. But why should he lie?

Why should Fergus Jopling look so upset at the sight of his photo and collapse and why should this young man be in such curious situations, such as standing over the unconscious Marcia in an empty rotting house where nobody went? Or making a nuisance of himself to Belinda herself, in a darkened street near the hospital?

Suddenly fear filled her. She could see no way of getting away from him, other than by taking him by surprise. 'Oh, damn, I've left it behind after all!' she suddenly exclaimed, her hand searching her pocket. 'Sorry, excuse me, got to go back,' she said, and turned and ran, her head down.

It was no use. She heard his footsteps pounding behind her. But mid-way between her and the distant gates of the hospital, she saw Adam Elliott, in casual clothes, walking towards his car. He looked up and hurried towards her, and as before, the young man melted away. She hurled herself into Adam's arms, unthinking. 'Oh, I can't bear it!' she gasped, and she was trembling all over. 'Where is he? Did you see him?'

Adam had only been aware that a man had been running after Bel. He had not looked at the face. Her heart sank.

'Where were you going?' he asked her, gently, but rather formally.

'Oh, I don't know. Out. Walking. Had to think. Honestly, I had no idea that I should be expected to–' she began, as she pushed back her dark hair, the half formed intention of now telling Adam everything taking shape in her mind. He was off duty, going out in his car. An overwhelming urge to be with him, a long way from the hospital, arose in her throat, almost choking her. But something in his constraint made her look more closely at him, and then at his car, and for the first time she realised that he was not alone. Hope Kingston sat in it. She was looking ahead, it was true, and not at Belinda and Adam, but there was a half smile playing around her mouth, a smile of malicious amusement.

Belinda felt as if she could kick herself, and Adam too. So it was true, what everyone said. So why was he always trying to persuade her that he was free and wanted her to confide in him? She flung away from him. 'I'm sorry. Why didn't you say–' she began, angrily. 'Oh, there's a taxi. That'll do,' and she did what to her was an unprecedented thing, and hailed the cab. Well, if she was now in the curious position of having been willed a fortune, she told herself grimly, she didn't have to walk to her own danger, when there were cabs around, and she didn't have to be dependent on people like Dr Elliott.

She sat in the back of the cab. She had told the driver to go to the station, for want of a better thing to say. But what she wanted was a telephone to contact her father; not to worry him with this latest thing that had happened, nor to tell him she was committing herself to marry a crippled embittered young man because of Penny. No, what she wanted and must have was Penny's telephone number.

But her father was still out and the taxi driver was still waiting, so she gave him Gilbert Orr's address. The smart flat he had mentioned.

Gilbert Orr was in, alone, and drinking a whisky with evident enjoyment. He looked tired, she thought. 'Are you likely to have to rush out or admit visitors in?' she asked oddly. 'Because I have just spent my last coppers on a taxi fare to here and...'

He had come to the door with his drink in his hand. He took Bel's hand and drew her in, putting down his drink on a table in the small hall, and as he shut the door behind her, he said, 'I was enjoying a bit of peace and quiet, and no, I do not expect visitors this evening, and you look as if you've been in another rough-house. Come and join me in a drink.'

He pushed her gently into the sitting-room. She had anticipated, if she'd thought about it at all, a more flamboyant taste. This room was mellow, designed with discretion, furnished with taste, and it had a profusion of books on shelves. A surprising room for someone like Gilbert Orr.

'Sit,' he invited, so she let her legs give way, and dropped exhaustedly into a huge leather upholstered low chair, which would have held two of her. She took the drink, wrinkled her nose at the smell of the spirit, but obediently drank it because he insisted. 'Now, take your time, and tell me everything.' He pulled a face at the way she looked up at him. 'I know it's the wrong man and the wrong place, but evidently you couldn't think of a better on the spur of the moment.'

'Oh, Gilbert,' she said, unthinkingly using his name.

'I like that,' he said, with satisfaction. 'Come on, who scared you? And don't be afraid of admitting to being scared. It'd make you more human.'

'It's not like me,' she admitted. 'I don't scare easily. But I've had two or three shocks since I saw you, and … my pride seems to have vanished, too. I would have been all right if I could have got my father on the telephone. But I couldn't. I expect he's out at a confinement. And I don't know what to do.'

'That chap been harassing you again? I

should have bashed him but he slipped off too quickly. I never did get told who he was, did I? I think I've seen his ugly face somewhere.' He thought for a bit. 'I know! In Calder's, the photographer's – it was in the window one week. Then it vanished.'

Belinda looked at him. He was a shrewd businessman. What would he say to the very odd story she tried to offer to Adam, who was too uncomplicated to believe it? She decided to try.

'There was this patient, called Fergus Jopling,' she began. It had to be simplified because Gilbert was a layman, not unintelligent, but certainly without medical knowledge. 'He'd had an operation on his eyes. We hoped he'd regain his sight, but his general condition was so complicated and dodgy that we gave in to him on every count, which explains why we let him think he was getting the same nurse round the clock, which of course was impossible.'

'That usual?' Gilbert frowned.

She shook her head. 'He was a wealthy man, but there was more to it than that. Anyway, Penny's voice is like mine, as you know, so she took on the easy duties while I rested. Any actual nursing to be done, I did it.'

'I know. I heard all that from Penny. She told him fancy tales to keep him interested; you did the messy jobs she'd have died rather than even learn about.'

'What did she tell you she told him?' Belinda gasped. 'And when?'

'No, no, take it in rotation. You tell me your side, I'll tell you what I know from that talkative little wretch of a sister of yours. Heaven,' he said unexpectedly with an unrepentant grin, 'provides us with the comfortable women we can't do without, and also the entertaining women which are also essential. You and your sister both. Pity I can't marry the pair of you,' he finished outrageously.

She got up, indignant, but he pushed her down again. 'I'll be good. Now, continue. The chap discovered he was being cheated, I suppose?'

'Yes, but I didn't know until very recently. He guessed somehow but he didn't mind. Why should he? He'd extracted from Penny the promise that she'd marry his nephew, and as an experienced fully qualified nurse she'd look after him for life. Penny took the precaution of giving him my name, and raised a furore with me to keep that promise.'

'And of course you agreed.'

'Yes, but somehow I never caught on that marriage was involved. I got the idea that a permanent nurse was all that was required.'

He looked surprised, murmuring, 'You didn't work it out that it was more than that?' so Belinda said impatiently, 'The whole thing was riddled with difficulties. He showed me that photo of the good-looking young man and I made the wrong comment about his nephew, that was evident. So I shut up – it was like walking on glass. Don't upset the patient, don't let him know of Sister's plot, don't let him worry, just wait till we take off his bandages. Well, we did, and he could see, and he was upset because I hadn't got Penny's colouring. But that passed off all right somehow, and I thought I was in the clear.'

He grinned. 'Fancy! With a young sister like young Penny!' which she ignored.

'Other things have been happening. Penny got into this mess with you and she didn't want to be a nurse and kept on at my parents, only...' She frowned. 'For reasons of her own she told them I was involved with marrying a patient and in case you don't know that, some hospitals (ours in particular) regard that as Crime No. 1. Well, I happen to love nursing and I didn't want trouble. I tell you, I've been worried sick, not knowing where to turn, nobody to discuss this with – well, my best friend has her own problems just now – she's filled with excitement about suddenly getting engaged. I wouldn't want to spoil that. Oh, Gilbert, I did think you could help me with that rather acrid line of conversation of yours and your shrewdness and common sense. Oh, I haven't made it sound very nice, have I, but I really do value those qualities in you!'

'Now you're talking!' he said, speculation in his glance. Then he grinned, shrugged, and said, 'Not to panic! I know it doesn't mean a damn thing. You're in love with someone else, aren't you? Well, think I haven't lived all these years without being able to *tell* when a girl's in love, and not with me?' He smiled wryly. 'What happened about this new Casualty Officer? And don't ask how I know. I'll tell you in a minute.'

'He thinks he's still my steady, and won't believe it's all over. He's in love with that girl who was in your attics. She's very ill, you know. I get the queer feeling she isn't going to "do". (Survive, I mean). Oddly that good-looking young man was standing over her, in the attics. And he's worried about her condition but assures me she won't die. He *says* she fell and hurt her head. Funny, if a person isn't in medicine they never give a qualified person the credit for that instinctive feeling abut what happened. I get the feeling he hit her, to knock her down. Why?'

Gilbert got up and looked very serious indeed. 'You mean he was keeping her there for his own purposes?'

She looked up, startled. 'I never thought of that! But as you mention it, I suppose I do. You see, did I tell you about the note I was supposed to have written to Derek, sending for him? Someone copied my writing, and fetched him down from the Midlands, then he said he didn't come specially to help me out in my trouble but to see a man about Marcia, who had disappeared. Then he said he had a letter from Marcia saying she was all right.' She shrugged. 'You guessed! Marcia took him from me, years ago, when we were going steady, then he came back to me, and she got him back again. I got fed up and opted out. He can't believe I've outgrown him.'

'Did you send such a note, Bel? I wouldn't have thought you'd do that.'

'Of course I didn't! Now he says he knows who did it, but won't tell me.'

'To my simple mind,' he said at last, 'all these things are tied up together. And you won't like it, but I believe your young sister's at the bottom of it all. Now why don't we take her to this Fergus Jopling and make her tell him everything, to release you from that promise—'

'Well, I wouldn't, anyway, even if I could find Penny. Oh, I know where she is but I haven't the telephone number and to fetch her here would be to worry Mummy, who's getting over a bad patch, healthwise. Besides, Penny won't say what she doesn't want to. One has to chance getting an untrue story, anyway. And another thing, it's all too late. The patient died, suddenly, and I find

I'm not only to marry his nephew, but I have the handling of all the estate, the whole of the vast fortune he built up, and it seems I'm not to let the nephew have any of it.'

Gilbert Orr looked blankly at her, then frowned in sheer puzzlement. But after taking a turn or two about the room, he suddenly finished his drink and burst out laughing.

'It's no laughing matter!' Belinda told him severely. She got up. 'I knew I shouldn't come to you in the first place!'

'Then why did you?'

'You were my last hope,' she said frankly. 'I can't tell my parents. My best friend is occupied with her own affairs. Besides, it's not fair to put the burden of all this mess on to the shoulders of other staff at the hospital.'

'Because one of them might think it right to do what you should have done at the start, Bel – gone to your Matron?'

She coloured. 'I deserved that. Yes, in the ordinary way I would have done, but all this has so many ramifications. In the first place, our hospital is trying to change, go modern – and in the process our dear old Matron/ nurse complex is fast vanishing, because Matron is getting bogged down with admin- istration. She'll soon be a glorified Civil Servant or secretary, and not the old aunt figure we used to know. And besides, as it concerns the ward sister too, that stops whispering in Matron's ear. And no, I can't go to the ward sister – because, besides being too busy to listen to all these details, she also would hear other people's secrets.' She was thinking about Dr Elliott, and about that cousin of his and his relationship with Hope, and if Dr Elliott himself was really about to be engaged to Hope, that would be another obstacle.

'I know it must be true about Hope Kingston,' she murmured, half to herself, 'because even that patient in the terminal ward said Hope was about to be ... no, she didn't. She jumped to the conclusion I was talking about Dr Elliott and said he was already committed elsewhere. But she must have meant Hope. I'm talking about a patient called Mrs Ivory,' she frowned, as Gilbert's eyebrows shot up.

'Mrs Ivory! She's ill in hospital?' he asked sharply. 'I didn't know that.'

'Do you know her, then?' Belinda asked, mystified.

'Yes, I know her,' he frowned, and laughter was a long way from his face now. 'Bel, sweet, I'm in property, remember? It was to me that they came about ... well let's just say a pretty big property. It fell through. Much water under the bridge. Come to think of it, it probably fell through because she was ill. What's the matter with her,

192

anyway? I mean, accident or illness?'

Bel, wrestling with the complication of her own thoughts, and half filled memories and wispy shreds of doubts and speculations, said absently, 'She's in a terminal ward. That means she won't recover. I don't think she knows that, mind. It's her eyes. She's almost blind.'

'Good heavens,' he muttered. 'Wouldn't you think that in that family at least, they wouldn't have eye trouble?' and as Bel looked at him in astonishment, he said, 'But you must know! How can you *not* know? She's Hope Kingston's mother – think, Bel! She's Sir Maxwell's own sister! And he's an eye bloke, isn't he?'

'Sir Maxwell's sister? Hope's mother?' she repeated. 'How can she be? Not the same name!' but he merely brushed that aside. 'Second, third husband – I forget which. Anyway, they came to me about this property, and Sir Maxwell said "My sister wants this or that", I forget what. Anyway, she was all thrilled and I was surprised that I heard no more about it. Oh, well, that explains it. Shame! She was a nice person. I liked her.'

'Well, so did I,' Belinda said savagely, 'and how come she has such a stinker of a daughter as Hope Kingston?' And as he laughed, she said, 'That isn't just cattiness, either. Dr Elliott has been trying to help me because … oh, well, I have to say it: my dear

193

young sister makes his life hell. He has her in lectures. Well, he had her. I bet he's glad she's given up nursing. Well, every time he tried to talk to me, that Hope Kingston was around, and I got the feeling he was going to be engaged to her. And she's so clever at putting me in an invidious position. Honestly, I can't think how she does it. She made him see me sitting in the car with you that night. Oh, yes, I smartly told him how you'd rescued me from...'

He laughed and interjected, '...a fate worse than death! No, I shouldn't laugh. To a girl like you, it would be a really bad thing to happen. But how much worse to have that damned Kingston woman start a rotten scandal about you? Bel, love, *couldn't* we? No, straight up, I mean marriage. I wouldn't expect *you* to want anything else! Heaven's, forget that little brute you're supposed to be marrying. It's an untenable promise and you know it! Of course you can't keep a promise you didn't make, and never mind about anyone else making it in your name!'

She looked flustered at him. 'You don't understand, dear Gilbert. You're so nice, but it isn't possible. I must go through with this, and even if I didn't, I couldn't marry anyone else. I've gone off marriage, somehow. By that, I mean I've gone off the idea of two people vowing to spend their lives together. It seems to me that there's strife everywhere

194

and no particular loyalty or devotion or anything...' She broke off and looked at her hands, bothered that she couldn't see them, her eyes were suddenly misty. She had been proposed to by a man who was decent and a prize for some girl, but not for her, because she had stupidly fallen in love with Dr Elliott, who even denied wanting to be her friend.

Gilbert Orr was just as embarrassed. It was the first time he had ever proposed marriage to any woman, and he suddenly realised how much he had wanted it, with Belinda Fenn. Marriage was not a thing he had thought about, before meeting her. Girls didn't expect it. Sleeping around was the usual thing, and it suited him, as it suited his girl friends. No ties, no dreary quarrels over domestic things. That was all in the far distant past, belonging to his childhood, when his parents had had constant up-heavals. Belinda Fenn got cross at times, but she didn't behave like a fishwife, and she loved people, even that young sister of hers, and if she showed irritation about Hope Kingston, well, Gilbert had seen Hope many times, and knew just how Belinda felt. But there was finality in Belinda's face.

He got up and said briskly, 'Well, that's that! Meantime your problems. We seem to have talked them out, but there's someone who can help from here onwards.' He put a finger on Belinda's lips to stop her protesting, and said, 'I want to show you something, and you are to swear you will count ten before you blow your top. I assure you everything's all right, and you'll bless me for this.'

'I don't trust you when you say things like that,' Bel whispered as he pulled her to her feet, so he laughed and said, 'Then I'll get my block knocked off for wanting to take you into my bedroom, I suppose, but that's where it is, what I want to show you,' and again he touched her protesting mouth. 'Come on, love, we still have a lot to talk about,' and he led her down the carpeted corridor of the flat to one of three doors. Bathroom, kitchen, and a room that was as tastefully furnished as the sitting-room, and as he threw open the door, she saw Penny lying there, fast asleep.

He covered her mouth with his hand, and almost at once someone came through from the dressing-room. Another woman. 'Now,' Gilbert said, 'this is Elizabeth, who lives with her husband in the next flat to mine, and who was going to stay with this young monkey all night, so just remember your manners and say hallo.'

'Didn't you tell her her sister was here until now?' Elizabeth scolded.

'We haven't had time to go into that,'

Gilbert snapped. 'We've had some heavy talking to do.' He turned to Belinda. 'She turned up on my doorstep just about worn out, earlier this evening. She'd thumbed lifts from where she was with her mother– *Will* you listen, Bel, love? No, her mother won't be worried because she thinks the little monkey's gone home to see Daddy. And her father won't know she isn't with her mother. The thing is, we've got her here now, and she's not going to get away without answering questions, as she would with you. Get me?'

Belinda nodded, suddenly weary. And she had, after all, to bless Gilbert Orr and his firmness. Elizabeth went back to her own flat while they talked. Penny looked adorably sleepy but rather apprehensive when she saw her sister. 'What are you doing here, Bel?' she asked, and a knowing look lit her eyes as she turned to Gilbert and back to her sister, so Gilbert said, 'Cut that out, Penny. It isn't like that, not like that at all. Just keep your mind on what I'm going to ask you, and I shall know if you're not telling the truth, and guess what I'm going to do if you don't?' He leaned against the doorpost. 'I'm going to your father, and when I'm through with him, you'll be back at the hospital, and Matron will be tipped off about keeping you under proper control.'

Penny looked mutinous. Belinda hadn't

realised how much her sister hated being at the hospital. She hadn't any great faith in Gilbert's methods, but they worked. With Penny ensconced between them in the sitting-room, assuaging her hunger with tea and toast, she reluctantly gave a lot of answers, which would have been more than a help if she'd given them before.

'All right. What do you want to know?' she muttered.

'Question 1: the name of the chap in the substitute photo. Quick, sharp!'

Penny hesitated, then shrugged. 'His name's Steve Rushton.'

'What's he do?'

'Loafs around. Oh, he wants to get in a show. That's what the photo was for.'

'And how is he keeping body and what he calls a soul together? Dole? Or sponging on his friends?'

'I don't know, honestly! He's getting cash from somewhere but I don't know where or how. Why should I?'

'Because you know him, that's why. Enough to help yourself to his picture. Don't give me that stuff about your friend's boy-friend being the photographer's son who helped himself to an unpaid copy. That won't wash. Come on now, the truth!'

Penny started to cry, decided it wasn't going to work with this new enraged Gilbert and said in a surly tone, 'Jill asked him for his photo to send in for a competition and he gave it to her. Well, I didn't know about it! I'd split my tea on Clive's photo and I knew the patient would be upset and that's all I'd had dinned into me: don't upset the patient! So when my friend Jill couldn't get any other picture the same size, I said get one from somewhere or I'll be sunk! So she did!'

'I see,' Gilbert said, turning it over in his mind. 'And how do you think he came by cash on which to live? Come on, you must have some idea!'

'I don't know!' Penny said wildly. 'Well, he did do a bit of photographers' modelling, and I think he said he was trying Begging Letters. I don't know how he did it and he didn't do it very well. He tried everything. He even served behind the counter in Will Byford's father's shop.'

'The chemist's?' Belinda ejaculated, and she and Gilbert exchanged startled glances, but Penny said quickly, 'There's nothing wrong in that. He sold veg behind a market stall one weekend and got paid half in veg and fruit. He'd do anything, anything. He's a sport!'

So that was it. Penny liked and admired him. Belinda felt a little sick. 'So you were sure he wouldn't mind you borrowing his photo for that purpose. But just why do you suppose the patient, just before he collapsed said "Monstrous!"? Why didn't he express surprise at a stranger's photo there?'

Penny shrugged. 'Because he wasn't a stranger. Steve drove the Jopling car at one time. Well, he took all sorts of jobs. And something went missing, and give a dog a bad name: poor old Steve got accused. He always had bad luck!'

'Penny, you've got it wrong! He's a bad man,' Belinda put in, anxiously.

Gilbert said, 'Never mind that, Bel. Let's get more information out of this young rip. Now Penny, think carefully: what was the plan for Belinda, that the patient talked over with you, thinking you were Belinda? The plan for his money?'

Penny's eyes were hastily lowered, but Gilbert must have known her very well. 'Look at me!' he thundered. 'And the truth, no fairy tales, because this involves the solicitors, and probably the police! So be careful!'

Belinda sat back in her chair. She felt he was going too far. Penny would never believe the police were likely to be called in. But Penny had a weight on her conscience and she was in the mood to be persuaded about anything, if they had but known. 'I didn't do anything wrong, honest! It's rotten of everyone to blame me, when all they kept saying to me was "Give in to the patient. Don't let him get upset. Give in to him about everything!" So I did. And look where it's got me.'

'What did he tell you, Penny?' Gilbert asked dangerously, so Penny gulped and said, 'I don't understand any of it. It was all big business. I got the feeling he thought our Bel was being wasted as just a nurse and he wanted her to go into big business and be a director and control vast companies, the lot. Well, it was so soppy, I just sat and listened and agreed with him. I'D BEEN TOLD TO!' she shouted, as Belinda was moved to protest. 'It was the same about the photo. I knew there'd be an awful row when they moved him and he asked to see that photo again and he'd blow his top again when he realised it was Steve's picture. I did think of telling him that Bel was going steady with Steve– Don't, Bel! Don't shake me! It was just an idea! But I didn't, because I had an awful piece of good luck. I went up to see his room after he'd been moved, with Clive's photo under my apron, meaning to just leave it, and that daft second year Colley was blinking through her thick glasses and cleaning up in there and I could see Steve's picture under the bed. Another minute and she'd have ripped off the mattress and seen it.'

'What happened?' Belinda asked wearily.

'I said in a loud voice that Sister was wanting Nurse Colley and I didn't know where she was, so the soppy thing came out and went haring down to Sister's Office, and

I nipped in and swapped the picture, and left the other one lying on the floor.' She giggled. 'Colley got in a row for spilling cleaning water on it and nobody realised it was my tea dried on. The clots!'

Penny was totally irrepressible, Gilbert saw in irritation. 'Never mind that. What happened to Rushton's picture?' so Penny said, 'I took that away, of course. It had caused enough trouble,' she finished primly. The understatement of the year, Belinda thought wryly.

But Gilbert hadn't finished. 'Was it you who told the patient that your sister was called "Lulie"?' and Penny's flushed face was answer enough. 'But how did you know?' Belinda asked sharply.

Penny wriggled and hedged but Gilbert was adamant. 'Oh, well, I got caught where I wasn't supposed to be, once,' she admitted at last. 'So I nipped into a phone booth, only they're open ones in the main hall of the hospital and I had to be telephoning someone so my friend Jill said, "Phone that gorgeous beast in Casualty" so I did. The new Casualty Officer – Derek Something. Only he thought it was you, Bel, and he said, "Is that you, Lulie? Not now!" So I said, "What are you calling me that for?" which was pretty dotty, but all I could think of to say. But my luck held. It appeared that you'd told him to stop calling you that, so he said, "Sorry, can't seem to get out of the old habit, and anyway, as we're going together again, what's it matter?" So I told the patient that was my name.'

'But why?' Belinda asked, in anguish.

'You don't listen,' Penny protested. 'He kept throwing scenes, and getting all beads of sweat on his face and forehead and it scared me so I just talked fast about any old thing, and when I said I was called Lulie (meaning you, of course) it stopped him being in a fret. It was always the same. Tell him something which was supposed to be about you, and he just stopped being in a pother and calmed down. That was how I came to tell him so many things.'

It had all gone too far and nobody had realised anything, and even Gilbert could appreciate how a young nurse like Penny, who hadn't much sense and was bored with the job and perhaps scared at the responsibility, would talk, about anything and everything, to get herself out of a fix.

'And now we come to the crunch,' Gilbert said, pouring himself out another drink. 'What you came here tonight for.'

Penny had thought everyone had forgotten that, and she was beginning to regret it herself. But she saw Gilbert meant business. So she thought fast, and said at last, 'Well, everyone thinks I'm rotten but I'm not all that rotten. Not really. I've been worrying about our Bel. I mean, I've seen Clive and I wouldn't like to be married to him. I wouldn't like him as a brother-in-law. Well, I thought I'd come up and talk to someone about what I knew, to see if our Bel could get out of that daft promise I made.'

It was, of course, though not the truth, a master stroke, but Gilbert didn't believe it, though he couldn't think what else the little wretch could have made that awful journey for, but the thing was, he could see that Belinda was swayed and impressed, and that he had lost ground here. He shouldn't have insisted on Penny giving them the reason for her appearance.

'So you think it's going to be all right now?' he said dangerously.

Penny eyed him anxiously. 'Well, yes, and the thing is, I thought that if I'd helped our Bel, then she'd help me,' Penny waited, while Belinda glanced at Gilbert, and said, 'Well, I will if I can, honey. How?' so Penny said delicately, while she examined her nails, 'You know I've always wanted to go on the stage and I've had an opportunity, only the thing is, Mummy won't have it, and Daddy lets her over-ride him, but if you told them that it was better for me to do something I would be good at and interested in, it would be better than forcing me to try and fail at something I didn't like, like nursing.'

Gilbert was about to explode. So that was

it! But Belinda's face stopped him from saying anything. Belinda looked scandalised, and Penny wondered how she could possibly have over-played her hand, for clearly she had. But Belinda was remembering someone's recent remark that Penny was a born actress and should have been on the stage, and together with that came the memory that Steve Rushton, with his good looks and lack of principle, also wanted the stage. For no reason at all, Belinda was suddenly very scared of Penny and Steve coming together. Beautiful in looks, and charming in their ways when they liked, the pair of them would be dynamite and a constant source of alarm for all those around them. She said crossly, 'I would never lift a finger to help you to get on the stage, and you are going back to Mummy tomorrow, and I will personally take you!'

Gilbert and Penny both gaped at her, though Penny could have told Gilbert and anyone else who might be interested, that the golden good nature of Belinda sometimes became swamped by an eruption of indignation and sheer fury if someone was unwise enough to push her too far. The thing was, Penny wondered, how on earth had she managed, with that innocent little speech, to push Belinda too far now?

Elizabeth, Gilbert's married neighbour, gladly offered to put Penny up for the night, just as Gilbert had said she would. She was a nice person and considered Penny was a sweet child whose wildness would go with time and understanding, and that both her sister and Gilbert Orr had read too much into her nonsense. Elizabeth therefore was not really equipped to look after Penny, and by the time the morning came, Penny was gone, leaving a note that she had returned to her mother so that her sister wouldn't have to take her, for if Belinda took her (Penny virtuously pointed out in the note) there would be a lot of trouble and her mother would be upset. Elizabeth was quite touched, and quite comfortable about the outcome, and felt that Gilbert Orr was unjustifiably angry when he heard the news.

Gilbert drove to the hospital, but although Belinda was still off duty between night and day turns, she had gone up to the wards.

Had she gone on duty voluntarily, he wondered? He sat in his car trying to work out what to do. The Fenn sisters were tricky, both of them, to say the least though Belinda didn't mean to be tricky; she was just independent and not likely to be swayed by other people's decisions. Even when she had asked his advice, she hadn't really looked crushed by the weight of circumstances, he recalled. She had just wanted someone's confirmation that she was doing the right thing, and it was a pretty big thing for someone like

Belinda, he saw.

Belinda, however, was not on duty, but had been sent for by the very sick Marcia. She was surprised. At no time had she and Marcia ever been on friendly terms. She went in a good deal of concern, wondering which of her loyalties would be stretched this time.

Marcia's eyes were ringed by dark hollows, and her voice a thread of sound but like Belinda she had plenty of determination and she wanted to say some things while she could. 'Sit close. Voice not strong,' she said, so Belinda sat right up to her head, on the stool from under the bed, and listened. Marcia began, 'Steve tried to kill me!'

The bald statement seemed to echo round the small room, which was no more than a glassed-in cubicle cut off from the main ward, and almost sound proof, the frosting of the glass giving maximum privacy, and used mainly for very sick patients who would be worried by the normal noises of attention on the ward. Belinda raised horrified eyes to Marcia.

Marcia said, 'You must believe me! I know too much about him.'

Belinda was a good listener. She just nodded. A string of questions would do more harm than good here. Marcia worried at the sheets with thin fingers, while she thought of what she must say. 'He's blackmailing someone.'

That handsome carefree young man, descending to blackmail? Belinda examined the idea, and found it wasn't too difficult when she recalled Penny's assertion that he had tried everything, even Begging Letters, in order to raise cash. So she contented herself by asking: 'Why?'

Marcia didn't want to say. She irritably shook her head. 'Listen! Hit-and-run driver. Steve knows who it is. I told him. Don't know why I did – had to tell someone.'

So, Steve was blackmailing the hit-and-run driver. Then he must be a wealthy man, to pay up. Into Belinda's mind came the memory of Steve tucking treasury notes into his pocket as he had come out of Sir Maxwell's room. Who had been in there, then? A wealthy patient – someone who was well-known enough to want to keep it quiet?

Marcia said, 'I was there. In the car. The driver didn't know I was there. Hid under a rug. Meaning to come out later. When it was too late for him to refuse. I liked him, you see.' She opened dark cavernous eyes to stare into Belinda's. Derek, their handsome new Casualty Officer, the hit-and-run driver? No, never! Besides, he never had a bean to bless himself with. Also, Derek would never be a hit-and-run driver. Whatever else he was or wasn't, he would do the right thing if he accidentally knocked someone down. He was a doctor, wasn't he? But weak, Belinda thought, her heart wrung with pity. And he had always loved Marcia.

Marcia promptly gave the lie to the thought of it being the almost teetotal Derek by saying baldly, 'Driver was drunk. Should have made him let me drive. He drove like the devil but when we got out into the country I thought it would be all right. Not much traffic. Then we saw a chap crossing from a car to a telephone box, and we couldn't stop. We hit him. He went down like a ninepin.'

She closed her eyes against the sight. 'No, no, don't stop me telling. I must. Might not get another chance.'

'What happened then?' Belinda asked gently.

'I kept hidden, then he pulled up and he kept saying "Did I hit someone? No, couldn't have!" And then he got out with a duster, looked at the front of the car, wiped the fender down and started to drive on again. I'd got out meantime. Softly closed the door. He was so fuddled he didn't hear me. Waited till he'd driven off again, then I ran back to that phone box and called the ambulance. No, didn't wait for it. Got myself home, somehow. Don't remember how.'

She was breathing fast. 'Head hurts,' she muttered, but she had more things to say and she had to say them. 'Bel, Steve mustn't know I told you. Kept me in attics in old house – Brotton Manor – sort of insurance, he said. Witness. The only witness. Didn't ask for big sums – just thirty pounds a week. Said that was the proper way to blackmail. No good asking for the moon.' She breathed fast. 'I wanted Derek. But he was away. In the Midlands. Had to get Derek down. No good writing as from me. Wrote as from you. Didn't mind, did you?'

'*You* wrote that note? But it was like my handwriting!'

'I know. Remembered it. Not too difficult. Funny "e" like a "3" backwards. Things like that. Thought he'd be intrigued enough to come. Thought I could get another note through. Would have, if your daft young sister had had any sense. Did call her, the night she came there, but she pretended to be afraid. Ran away.'

The astonished Belinda sat thinking this over. The explained how the letter had been signed 'Lulie' though the person writing it hadn't started it with the little name Belinda had called Derek. Of course, how was Marcia to know that pet-name? 'How did you manage to post it to Derek, as from me?' she asked.

'I wasn't tied up. Just locked in. Tied it to a stone and threw it down with a stamp on it. Trusted someone would post it. It fetched Derek only … you didn't know the rest of it. Couldn't contact you.'

'You should have made Penny listen,' Belinda said, but it was no good. Any knocking or sounds at Brotton Manor were automatically thought to be tramps. 'How did you know Derek called me "Lulie"?' she asked. She must know that. Marcia smiled twistedly. 'He absently called me Lulie once. Poor Derek. No finesse, but he would have helped me, if he could.'

'He's been so worried about you. But then he said he got a note from you saying you were all right.'

Marcia looked alarmed. Clearly she knew nothing of that. 'Steve,' she muttered. 'Typed it, probably. I think he knows ... I'll tell someone...'

'But you haven't told me who he's blackmailing? And for how long?'

'How long? Oh, since...' Marcia thought, calculated, then gave a date when it started. Belinda was so stunned she could only sit there and stare. That date was so significant.

Marcia looked past her and got panicky, trying to push her, make her go. A man's shadow was outside. He moved back as Belinda rose, and by the time she had got outside, there was nobody standing there. Who had it been, to frighten Marcia so? Belinda questioned other patients, nurses, if they had seen someone. Nobody had. Everyone was too preoccupied with their own affairs. It was a busy ward. But someone had been there… But who?

Belinda didn't scare easily, but what Marcia had told her had given her a bad shock. The date of the accident coincided roughly with the date when Clive Gregory had been knocked down, and his had been a hit-and-run accident. Could it be the same one? But if so, who then was Steve blackmailing? He had been chauffeur in the Jopling household so they would know him. And who could have knocked Clive Gregory down?

Belinda went to find Derek. 'Marcia sent for me,' she said.

It was his coffee break; together they gravitated to the canteen. People watching them wondered if the old romance was 'on' again. Both likeable young people. Adam Elliott heard someone say, 'It's almost like Fate, the way he's been sent back here again, isn't it?' but the other person said, 'Hardly, with Marcia still dangling for him. I'd have thought it better if Belinda Fenn had never seen him again.' Adam Elliott never discounted nurses' gossip. They knew all that was going on. That conversation chilled him.

He wished that Casualty Officer could have found someone else to take his coffee with. Adam had wanted to speak to Belinda himself. But as it was, they seemed to be discussing something serious enough, so he went to the Appointments Section to look up some details he wanted, and to see an old patient before he could hope Belinda would be finished with the Casualty Officer.

Derek was put out about Marcia sending for her. 'Now what would she do that for, Lulie? I hope she isn't stirring things up again because–'

'Derek, don't,' Belinda pleaded. 'I wasn't going to tell you but I think I must. She told me she had been held by force in that house.' She looked at the conflict in his face, and she said, 'She also told me she wrote that note.'

'Now what did she say that for?' he demanded.

'Hadn't you thought of her as the one? Well, I'll tell you briefly how it came about,' she said, and when Belinda wanted to be brief, she was brief. She made it sound rather cold, too, she thought, but she couldn't help it.

Derek said, 'This chap, Rushton, is it really possible he could be blackmailing someone? Holding Marcia as a *witness*? It sounds a bit far-fetched, doesn't it?'

'Does it? It seems to be happening all the time, according to the newspapers and TV,' Belinda said, rather bitterly. 'Too many people trying to force other people to do what they want. Never mind about whether I liked Marcia or not – it was a rotten situation to get into, and if only my young sister–' She broke off and bit her lip. It was all past now, and who could blame someone as young as Penny for running off if she heard a voice calling her at night from a lonely house? But something about that story wasn't right, surely, Belinda remembered. Penny went there at night, after dark, surely, and how could Marcia have seen her from the attics of that old house? Had there been a full moon?

Now she was filled with doubt, especially as Derek found it hard to believe. 'If the chap was holding her prisoner, is it likely he would have allowed her to escape with you people?' he asked sceptically.

'To be honest, I don't think he would have, if he hadn't heard us talking about fetching the ambulance. He must know that Mr Orr owns the property, and he also must know what the penalty is for keeping someone there against their will.'

'Then why didn't Marcia make a fuss, call the police about it? She hasn't, you know,' Derek pointed out. 'If you ask me, it's something she's in too, and she's trying to slither out of it by making it seem as if it's that chap's idea.'

'Why don't you go up and see her, find out from her if the story's the same,' Belinda suggested.

Derek played with his spoon, then he said, 'I suppose you'd think me pretty rotten if I said I was tired of her and didn't want her

214

any more? I'm sorry for her. Sorry she's in a poor state, as I heard she is. But she frightens me, the things she gets up to. Not exactly outside the law,' he said hurriedly, 'but definitely on the fringe, if you get my meaning. No, I think I'll let sleeping dogs lie. This chap Rushton may come and see her.'

'I think that's hardly likely,' Belinda started to say, and then she recalled the shadow of a man against the frosted glass of Marcia's cubicle. Suddenly she was reminded of Steve Rushton. Could it have been him? And was that why Marcia had been so anxious to push Belinda out, and not appear to be talking to anyone? Yes, it wasn't in Steve's interests for Marcia to talk, was it?

She stumbled to her feet. 'Where are you going in such a hurry?' Derek said.

'I've just thought! She said Steve Rushton had tried to kill her, and I believe it was him standing outside her ward, only he was gone by the time I had got out of her room.'

Derek stared at her. 'Oh, Lulie, don't be so dramatic. This is our hospital – sleepy old Spanwell General, where nothing ever happens, least of all someone getting in to try and do a patient a mischief. Sit down and let's discuss your sister Penny's part in all this. Now there is a thing that has been worrying me.' He pulled her down beside him again. 'There are people saying that you've been tricked into marriage with that

215

patient's nephew. Now that I cannot believe but now people are saying that your sister Penny started it, and now the patient has died, who shall say?'

'Please, Derek, don't talk about such things. It's all above board. I've only got myself to consider in this and I've promised to marry Mr Jopling's nephew and look after him all his life. Yes, it's true, and it's really nobody else's business.'

Derek said, 'So it really is true what they're saying! It's for all that money! Well, I advise you to duck when you go out because there are some reporters outside. Can you blame them? It isn't every day that a blind patient traps a nurse into marrying his bad-tempered nephew for the sake of being on the board of all his mines and companies; and a very rich young woman, and power-ful, at that!'

Belinda got to her feet, this time with pur-pose. She was white-faced. 'I have an itching palm, Derek, to chastise you for that insult-ing remark. Consider I've done it, and don't trouble to speak to me again,' she said between her teeth. He got to his feet as if to stop her, but she left him swiftly, slipping between other people, so that he couldn't catch her.

As she made for the stairs, Derek saw Dr Elliott fall into step beside Belinda. He didn't get a very good welcome either, Derek saw with satisfaction. But he was a rather puzzled young man as he went back to Casualty. He had merely blurted out his thoughts, on the surprising moment. Why should Belinda be so furious, considering the story was obviously true?

Adam Elliott said to Belinda, 'I'm sorry but I have to talk to you, Bel. Now!'

'Honestly, there isn't anything to say, Dr Elliott! I've tendered my resignation. Everyone knows I'm going to marry the patient, just as his uncle made me apparently promise to. What does it matter?' she asked in surprise as he threw up his head. 'It's my life! I shall probably make a very good go of it. And at least I shall be wanted by someone.'

'Don't *I* want you?' he asked savagely.

She stopped on the next landing and stared at him. 'No. Or you would have said so before, on all the many occasions when I referred to you as being half engaged to Miss Kingston. You never denied it.'

'It was too futile a thing to bother with,' she was amazed to be told. 'As if I'd have even thought of trying to help you at all, if I'd been engaged to someone else. What sort of person do you take me for?'

'But everyone said so.'

'Who is *everyone?* How I do dislike that expression!'

'Well, for a start, Mrs Ivory, and I'm just

going up to see her, as well as the other patient, Marcia, who used to be a nurse here. So please–'

'I believe you didn't realise Mrs Ivory was Hope's mother,' he said, arresting Belinda's headlong flight. 'Isn't it the most likely thing that that nice but unhappy woman would wish for her daughter to be engaged to someone she had known for a long time, someone she could trust to look after Hope? And I personally haven't got what it takes to tell her straight out to her face that I consider Hope as a very mean sort of girl whom I would never look at, even if I hadn't met someone who–' He made the familiar bothered gesture of rubbing his hand down the back of his head. 'Any use telling you that you're on my mind all the time, and I'm wondering (even when I'm trying my hardest to concentrate on a case) what on earth you are getting up to next?'

She looked so distressed, she took his mind off the speech he had been preparing, and which it wasn't much use trying to make, on this particular busy staircase. They stood with a bare foot of space between them, against the wall so that people could pass, and their faces mirrored their perplexity and distress. Belinda said softly, 'When I asked if you were my friend, you said you couldn't be, and I did want your friendship so much!'

'I don't think that that was exactly what I

meant,' he objected. 'What I actually said was–'

'You said in an angry voice that it wasn't friendship you were offering me. I wanted that,' she said, passionate entreaty creeping into her voice. 'I have to marry that young man in a few days' time. He's adamant about it, and demanding, and he dislikes me as much as I – oh, I shouldn't say that about a patient!'

It was too public a place. He said curtly, 'Come down to his ward. There's something I want to ask him, in front of you. Oh, Bel, if only we could have talked this over, quietly, but somehow everything becomes so heated!'

She almost pointed out that he hadn't helped in the past, but the depth of her wretchedness was too great to bother. She was trapped, at a time when it now occurred to her that people had not been telling her the truth about Hope Kingston but just voicing wishful thinking, and that he himself had been absolutely masculine in his inability to see the way a woman's mind would work in the circumstances. Clearly he didn't have any illusions about Hope and he gave Bel the credit for realising that, and for sharing his own clear thinking about her. He would have been shocked if he had known how Belinda rated all men in the presence of an experienced operator like Hope Kingston. Belinda was quite certain that the pressure of his future career, the burden of his cousin Oswald Vaisey to cope with, and the fact that he liked Hope's uncle very much, were all enough for him to capitulate and marry Hope in the end, as the most natural and civilised thing to do.

The patient was at his most truculent when they stopped by Clive Gregory's bed. He glared at them both and said sharply, to Belinda, 'Where have you been? I've had them running about all over the place looking for you – or so they said! You know I wanted to talk to you!'

'Well, I'm here now,' Belinda said quietly. 'And Dr Elliott wants to say something to you as well.'

Clive's arrogance allowed him the merest glance in Dr Elliott's direction. He said to Belinda, 'I've arranged the wedding. At the private chapel at home. Get something decent to wear but don't run up outrageous bills. No need for that. Go at once. I want to see what you've bought to wear, in case I don't like it.'

Dr Elliott stood quietly looking at him, while Belinda said, in some surprise, 'I don't have to buy anything. I've got a nice outfit. And why rush today – we have three days.'

'No, we haven't, and if I say buy something new, I mean it!' Clive snapped. 'I am going home today. I'm tough. Having been through two road accidents, I am not likely to crumple under any others. My chauffeur is driving me home.'

Belinda thought, with shock – he must be tough! How many other young men, having been in an accident like the first one, could stand up to tangling with another, and be ready to leave hospital so soon to be married? But Clive couldn't believe that he wasn't going to get his hands on the money. His remark confirmed that. 'I am going home today to see my legal men about that crazy Will, so don't get ideas about being the one in possession. Something must be done about that!'

Dr Elliott said, breaking smoothly and quietly into the conversation, 'I think you are under a misapprehension, Mr Gregory, about a lot of things. In the first place, Nurse Fenn wasn't the one to make that promise to your uncle: it was her young sister, who made it in Nurse Fenn's name – a very wrong thing to do, but a promise that won't stand up. Please!' he said quickly to Belinda, who had tried to break in, shocked and angry, because she hadn't expected him to do this. 'Also you cannot leave hospital until I say so. Did they not tell you? In my opinion you are not fit to go, not for at least another week. If you wish, you can conduct your legal business from here. You know you are free to have as many visitors as you like, after lunch. Lastly, Nurse Fenn isn't free to marry you.'

'Please!' Belinda urged again, in an agonised voice, but this merely served to convince the patient of the truth of what Dr Elliott had said.

'Well, from what I hear, *you* are not free to marry her, either,' he said dryly, and dismissed the matter. His churlish young face took on a mask of boredom which was difficult to batter through, as he said crushingly, to Belinda, 'And in case you have a lot of reasons why you can't go and buy those clothes, I've already found out from the ward sister that you have three days off, between duties. And your young sister has gone home, so she can't make any more tiresome situations to be unravelled,' and he indicated that that was the end of the discussion, so far as he was concerned.

Whatever Dr Elliott had been going to say, he now appeared to consider worthless as a working point of argument. He took Belinda's arm, squeezed it to stop her from struggling away from him, and marched her to the door. As they left the room they both turned. His holding of Belinda's arm in that easy possessive manner had produced on the patient's face such a look of fury that for the very first time, Belinda was frightened of what she was doing. 'So now he knows I meant what I said and that he's on a losing wicket,' Dr Elliott said quietly, with satisfaction.

Belinda walked beside him, dazed. Around them the life of the hospital went on. Patients were being pushed by porters on trolleys up to the wards, or to the theatre; nurses pushed wagons of clanking cups and jugs of milk and coffee; another nurse rushed along with a bunch of flowers, in search of a vase, a harassed expression on her face; and a couple of juniors staggered under a load of linen for a bed suddenly being made up for an emergency. Two housemen strolled by, their stethoscopes swinging, their faces carefree; the ward sister, her face far from carefree, attempted to hurry from her office, but was again recalled by the urgent summons of the telephone on her desk. This was a normal hospital day, but to Belinda it was suddenly all different. She felt unsure of herself. She hadn't even felt like this when the late Fergus Jopling's lawyers had made it painfully clear to her what the full content of that unfortunate promise had really been. No, the thing, the scintillating thing binding her, was the fact that Dr Elliott, in his usual mundane yet shattering manner, had made it clear to her that he was in love with her and that she and she alone was the woman he wanted to marry, and no amount of patients, however truculent and wealthy they might be, should stand in his way.

He glanced down at her, half smiling, and his eyes held hers, just as if there was nobody else near. He said, 'Belinda?' and she said, a little breathlessly, 'You really want me to believe that it's me ... and not Hope or anyone else? You really mean that?'

'That's about it,' he said, one eyebrow going up at a lopsided angle which made his half smile frankly comical.

It was not time to be comical, she thought fiercely. 'How do you know I feel the same way about you?' she asked fiercely on a low note, because people were still all around them.

'Can see it!' he said laconically. 'It sticks out all over you! It had better, too!' he added darkly, and again took her arm, guiding her towards the stairs to the Terminal Ward. 'I decided, after I'd heard our young Gregory friend in action, that I would reserve my comments there and talk instead to Hope's mother. Oh, come on, Bel, she likes you! She told me so.'

'Yes, but ... her daughter...'

'You're frankly intimidated by Hope, aren't you? I really wouldn't have thought you'd be intimidated by anyone!' he marvelled.

'I am not intimidated by Hope!' she stormed. 'I am totally unwilling to upset Hope's poor mother, who quite misguidedly adores her daughter and seems to see her as a different person from ... the one I see.'

'Well, she likes you, and if I tell her, she'll accept it. I'm going to tell Sir Maxwell, too, in case he's harbouring a wrong idea in that direction.'

So Belinda accepted it and went quietly upstairs with him, wondering where all this was going to end, and wishing that she didn't feel so queer and shaky and excitable inside.

But they didn't manage to see Hope's mother after all. Nobody was being admitted to her bedside except Sir Maxwell, and as they waited outside the door, Belinda wanting to go away but Adam waiting to hear what had suddenly gone wrong, Sir Maxwell came out.

Well, it was a Terminal Ward. It said so above the door. But somehow Mrs Ivory had looked so ... well, not ill, Belinda thought confusedly. And she had been so excited about the gadget Sir Maxwell was going to send up to her, to enable her to see, however imperfectly, the pictures in the cat book. Now one glance at Sir Maxwell's face told Belinda that the cat book would no longer be wanted, nor the gadget with which to see those coloured plates. Mrs Ivory had died, and Sir Maxwell looked almost as if he were reeling under the shock.

At first he didn't recognise them, then Adam, who was just as tall, standing directly in his path, and murmuring sympathetic remarks because he knew what Mrs Ivory had been suffering from, made his presence known.

Sir Maxwell looked as if he were making an effort to think of something to say, instead of brushing aside the appropriate sentiments from a colleague. He said at last, with a curious lightening of his face as if he were throwing off a burden, 'Well, she's gone now. And now I shan't have to … any more,' but what it was he wouldn't have to do any more, the other two didn't catch. Adam thought he meant he wouldn't have to bear the weight of guilt because he had failed with his operation on his sister's eyes, but he thought this was a wrong attitude to take, because Mrs Ivory had malignant growths in other parts of her body. Belinda thought he meant that he wouldn't have to suffer from his sister's delight in the things she liked, and her inability to accept that she wouldn't have them for long.

Sir Maxwell walked between them both, leaving them standing there looking down at him, as he half stumbled down the staircase to the clinic he was supposed to be taking, but all Sir Maxwell could think of was that he would no longer have to pay a blackmailer for keeping the news from his beloved sister that her precious son had been a hit-and-run driver.

TEN

Gerald Orr sat waiting outside the hospital. He asked a passing nurse about Belinda and learned that Belinda had been sent for to see a very sick patient although she wasn't actually on duty. Gerald Orr waited, and then he spotted the reporters. He had no wish to be caught up with publicity nor did he think it would help Belinda, so he quietly drove away. He would have to think of some other way of contacting her.

So he missed seeing Hope and Lloyd arrive at the hospital. They had been sent for. Sir Maxwell and their mother were twins; always very close. Hope and Lloyd had been more close to each other than to their mother. They stood by the bedside, helplessly looking at her. With her eyes closed, she looked serene and remote but somehow young again. No longer the woman with failing sight, who was always pressing for Hope to marry Adam Elliott and for Lloyd to make a good marriage so that he wouldn't be in continual trouble over money. How his mother had always seemed to be *au fait* with news of his escapades, Lloyd couldn't think but miraculously she had not found out about the one thing that he had done which always bedevilled him. What would happen if anyone ever found out?

So, although they had been warned of the shortness of their mother's prognosis, they stood helplessly by the bedside, wondering what to do next. Their careful upbringing made them both say all the right things to the ward sister and the nurses, and they stayed just the right time, and quietly left. But somehow, her passing had left them feeling strangely insecure.

'What do we do now?' Lloyd asked blankly.

'Don't ask me to see Uncle Maxwell for you,' Hope said, between her teeth. '*I* haven't done anything, but he makes me feel as guilty as hell!'

'Perhaps he knows about your being pally with that greasy little Oswald Vaisey,' Lloyd said nastily.

Hope didn't bother to answer. She didn't know what she saw in Oswald. He was no good. He was perpetually getting her brother into money troubles. It had been through worrying about Oswald's pressures that had made Lloyd take his mind off the road that night, she was sure. Hope didn't know he'd gone as far as to get drunk, nor did she know that Marcia Peters had been in the back of his car on that occasion under the rug. Lloyd himself hadn't known that. But he guessed that something of the sort had happened, for

Lloyd had asked her such odd questions afterwards, such as if one would know if one had knocked someone down, and what the procedure was. He had looked so ill. She had been afraid, and had let him talk it out of his system and finally drop into a heavy sleep in an armchair. Hope shivered, remembering.

A nurse stopped to commiserate with them. All the nursing staff had liked Mrs Ivory. Hope's eyes were chill as she stiffly thanked the girl for her condolences, then Hope and her brother passed on through the hospital.

Steve Rushton was with Sir Maxwell. He had called a second time in one week. 'Sorry, sir,' he said, with those polished manners of his, 'but I have a few extra expenses this week and I could do with a bit more cash. Also I had the idea of raising the amount of the sum, and making it monthly, too; save bothering you so often. Besides, inflation being what it is...'

His easy manner slipped a bit, as he realised that Sir Maxwell wasn't making his usual pretence of getting out his instruments to look in Steve's eyes this time in case the nurse came in. He just sat looking at Steve as if he had never seen him before.

Steve said urgently, 'Sir ... the cash, if you please?'

Sir Maxwell seemed to bring himself back to the present. 'There won't be any more cash forthcoming,' he said quietly, and turned to his papers, at the same time calling, 'Nurse, next patient, please!'

Steve said, 'Just a minute! I don't think I quite understand!'

Sir Maxwell said, 'The person I was protecting by paying for your silence, is no longer with us. So I don't give a damn what you do now. Good morning!'

He nodded to the nurse, who showed Steve out, and began to bring in a small dumpy woman who could hardly see to find the chair. Steve stood irresolute, his jaw dropping; caught in the swift-moving throng of a full day of clinics. Nobody had any time to spare, nobody cared whether he threatened to tell anyone the secret he held. Nobody cared a jot. He stood stupefied. It had been an income for life, he had thought. What had gone wrong?

He just couldn't believe it. He felt such an amateur. He tried to think quickly but he was too stunned. Marcia! It was all her fault! He decided to slip upstairs and see her. He should have gone into her room yesterday, but it had unnerved him, seeing that Fenn girl with her. A friend of Sir Maxwell's family, he thought angrily. He had seen Belinda Fenn once, standing by Hope's car, talking to Hope and to Dr Elliott. He knew that there was some story about her and a rich patient, too.

A policeman came into Casualty. For a moment Steve went cold and his scalp prickled. If Sir Maxwell really wasn't bluffing, could he have called the police? It was an indictable offence, Steve suddenly recalled, blackmailing. But would Sir Maxwell say at this point that someone had been blackmailing him for some time, and to admit that he had been quietly paying up for so long? After all, Sir Maxwell, to be ethical, should have called the police to that nephew of his instead of paying someone to keep the crime quiet, surely?

His old confidence returned to Steve Rushton. He doubted if Sir Maxwell would make such an admission. But how was it that he was only protecting that nephew of his and not Lloyd's sister. And how had Lloyd died?

That was a thought, but one which vanished on the instant for Lloyd at that moment walked through Casualty, having tried to see his uncle for more cash and been curtly told to stop bothering him during a clinic. Lloyd was flushed and surly. So it hadn't been true, then! Steve moved across, meaning to speak to Lloyd, then Sister Casualty forestalled him, stopping to speak to Lloyd herself. Steve heard her say how sorry she was to hear that Lloyd's mother had died. So that was how it was! It had been Lloyd's mother who was being protected.

231

But didn't Sir Maxwell care about himself and the rest of his family? Well, if he didn't now, he would soon, Steve promised himself.

Steve slipped upstairs to Marcia's ward with a lighter heart. But it was no use: they wouldn't let him speak to her. She wasn't so well today, he was told. But he knew Marcia had seen him. She had raised her head and pure terror had filled her face at the sight of him. Well, perhaps she would be more receptive to talk to him when he did get in to see her. Meantime, he must think.

He went outside, and saw the press boys were trying to get in. Sometimes Spanwell General admitted them. Today they were not being admitted, and no reason was being given. Steve wasn't to know that Dr Elliott was protecting his own. He had seen them, but he didn't know that Gerald Orr had been waiting to see Belinda. Belinda hadn't got round to telling him about Gerald Orr, nor had she told him half the things that she had told Gerald. There had been no time.

Adam Elliott had arranged to take Belinda to lunch, when he could get off duty. He had left her to go back and get some rest. She had looked curiously white and strained. He wondered if it was Mrs Ivory's death, so soon following that of Fergus Jopling, but he discounted this. Belinda was a qualified nurse, and had seen death too many times. Both of those deaths had been patients, not close friends. He stood still, thinking. There must be a lot she hadn't told him. He recalled that he hadn't heard anything about that young sister of hers.

He half decided to go back and speak to her about it, but he was called into Casualty, and sucked into the maelstrom of hospital emergencies. They flared up and died down. One moment it was quiet, all going according to plan; the next all was chaos. This was an explosion in a nearby factory. It was thought to be gas. He joined the rest of the staff who could be spared to converge on Casualty and help.

The press boys found something to console them here, and when they were turned out, Steve Rushton, his mind made up, offered them another story, for cash on the nail. Steve told them about Lloyd and his hit-and-run accident, and for good measure he told them about the number of cheques Lloyd had forged.

The addition to the story killed it. Steve knew when he wasn't being believed. They wanted proof. Sir Maxwell walked through Casualty at that moment, and they stopped to nail him.

This was better. Steve, grinning confidently, listened to them ask the question: was it true that his nephew Lloyd had knocked down and injured a man and not reported it? Sir Maxwell said, not batting an eyelid, 'So far as I know, my nephew is a poor driver, but that is all I am aware of!' and he walked on. The press boys liked him and weren't pleased with Steve. 'Get proof next time,' they advised him. They, too, had jobs to keep.

'I've got proof,' he said angrily. 'Think I hadn't? The proof is in Ward 17, Women's section. A little redhead just inside the ward, in a cubicle of her own. She was in the car at the time (hidden under a rug on the back seat) and she's aching to tell someone!'

He watched them surge upstairs. If it was true, he would get his cash as they came down. With a bit of luck the ward sister would be at coffee, and the press had already been cleared at the door to come in and be told about the gas explosion. Steve wondered what he would be paid for that.

He wasn't very happy. He felt he wasn't handling the thing like a big operator. He went and had a cup of tea, at a counter which commanded a view of the main stair-case down which the press boys would have to come. He tried to make his brain work but it seemed sluggish today. He could, he supposed, report Sir Maxwell to his superiors, or to the board of the hospital, but he knew he wouldn't get paid for the information. He supposed he could sell the story to a Sunday paper, but it wouldn't have to be one of the top flight ones. Sir Maxwell probably had shares in them, for all he knew. He pushed his mind here and there to find some way out of it. He had knowledge, but couldn't sell it. What was the good of a secret if you couldn't cash in on it?

Two young nurses were talking near at hand. They were in Penny's set. Their young voices, clear but pitched low, penetrated his thoughts, made planning impossible. He gave up and listened. 'She's awful! She came back to him and she was in his flat and her sister went there and found her and there's supposed to be nothing in it but everyone knows that Gilbert Orr is an absolute, well, you know what I mean! I can't think how it was that Penny didn't get thrown out of this hospital before!'

'Who was letting her in at night? How come no one ever found out?'

'Could be that her sister was so well in with that rich patient who left her everything. Now there's a peculiar thing. She says she doesn't want to marry that nephew of his but I don't believe–'

'Not the one who was crippled through that hit-and-run business? But he's horrible – he always looks so bad-tempered and sneering sort of thing.'

'He *is* bad-tempered. He *does* sneer. All the time. Even Sister Cas. said so, the day he

235

was brought in from that other accident. I wouldn't marry him, not for two fortunes, but that Belinda Fenn is going to! I've heard it on the best authority–' but the other girl noticed belatedly Steve's interest and hushed her friend. They had been talking in low tones, but he had moved gradually nearer to them. And now he had another bit of information. Belinda Fenn was going to be so rich. Through marrying Clive Gregory. Well, how could he prise some of that lovely cash away from her, he wondered? He sat staring into the middle distance, thinking of ways and means. If she was going into that marriage hating it, it must be for her young sister's sake. How would it be to touch her for cash in order not to divulge what Penny had been up to? Say, Penny had been the one to be in the car at that time? Who was to say she hadn't? And then, how about touching Clive Gregory for ... what could he be touched for? The name of the hit-and-run driver? Everyone knew he wanted revenge. He should pay well for it. He missed the press boys, so deep was his plotting, but it wouldn't have helped him. They hadn't got the story he had sent them to get, but another one. The redheaded girl they had gone up to try to see, had been being brought back into the ward from the fire staircase, where she had fallen, and injured her back, trying to escape from the hospital. 'Don't let Steve Rushton get me!' she had been pleading when they had been bringing her back to her bed. 'Don't let him!' her hysterical voice followed the press boys.

Telling Adam about all the things she had told Gilbert Orr, was curiously much more difficult, Belinda found, as she faced him over the lunch table that day, in a quiet but very good hotel on the way to Cheppingstock. Not the one they had gone to before, she was glad to note, and one which didn't have Hope and Lloyd at another table.

But Adam was Adam. She was scared he wouldn't like Penny any more than Gilbert had, but Gilbert Orr didn't matter to her, and Adam did.

'Now let's not spoil a good lunch,' Adam said, smiling. 'Let's eat first, and if anyone comes up and says they know us, we'll leave, so don't worry,' a remark which brought a quick flush to her cheeks. She knew he was referring to Hope. 'But after lunch, I think we'd better make a completely fresh start and tell each other everything, don't you?'

'I've got a load on my conscience, but I shouldn't think you have!' she said.

'Oh, I don't know,' he sighed. 'I can't pretend to be ignorant of what my cousin, Oswald Vaisey, has been getting up to over the years. When I've known, I've bailed him out, but after what you told me you'd over-heard, I asked my solicitor to look into things for me. He's a good chap. We were at school together. He knew Oswald, and he promised to be discreet. The result was not good. What do you do with a chap like Oswald? In the good old days, there was always some reliable uncle who owned a plantation with a rotten climate, to which the blighter could be dispatched. Not any more, though.' He smiled and spread his hands. 'You do realise, Bel, that you won't be rich if you marry me? Comfortably off, not rich. Perhaps we shan't be comfortably off for long.'

'What do you mean, Adam?'

'Oswald might need baling out again. Things like that.'

Things like that, Belinda thought wildly. Did he mean that Penny, too, might need to be baled out, at a cost? Her heart quickened its beats. What would he say when she told him that Penny was in the care of neigh-bours of Gilbert Orr? Suddenly she had an overwhelming desire to tell him everything and chance what he thought, so she did. She talked composedly while she ate, and hid nothing. She could see that he didn't like her friendship with Gilbert Orr, and he looked predictably angry when he heard she had made a confidant of the man.

'If I had known how you felt about me,' she said, looking suddenly up at him in a way that made his pulses race, 'I wouldn't have gone near Gilbert Orr. I would have come to you to confide in. But I had to have a friend to talk things over with. And I must say he's been very decent, and considering the way Penny played him up, he's behaved very well. He has said repeatedly that he's no angel, but in his way he's rather nice, kind. No frills. Terribly down to earth, and he's really quite stern with Penny and she minds him.' Belinda shivered. 'But I can't help feeling that something quite horrible is going to happen, yet I can't think why.'

'It's because things have personally quickened their tempo for us, these last few weeks,' Adam soothed. 'Bel, you're not going through with your promise, are you? Surely not?'

She half shook her head. 'I would have thought I could say, out of hand, without thinking about it, yes, I am going to keep my promise. But then, it wasn't a promise of mine. I mean, quite apart from Penny having made it in my name, it was not a promise I would have made. How awful to be young and untried and snatching at the easy way out of things, as my sister Penny did! I would have firmly refused to make such a promise and called Sister. I wonder why she didn't? I wonder why she didn't tell me sooner, but just went on hoping for the best, hoping the worry would go away?'

239

Adam nodded. 'And that is my biggest worry of all, that your sister Penny is like that. All her life she'll be like that. Isn't there some decent chap, a doctor, for instance, that your father could get her married off to? Well, it's in his interest, isn't it? He won't want her to be a thorn in his side for the rest of his life, will he?'

Or a thorn in our sides, Belinda thought, with sharp anxiety, as she allowed herself a peep into a future married to Adam Elliott. A future in which she hoped to be allowed to continue her nursing.

'All the men who have wanted to marry Penny since she was seventeen are sober people who couldn't hope to keep her interested, or to hold her down,' Belinda recalled. 'The local chemist who makes up Daddy's prescriptions, and the new vicar. Not the best people to be worried by my young sister. But they both were in love with her. My mother noticed it.'

'And I hope had the sense not to mention it to Penny?' and Belinda nodded abstractedly. But Belinda, who was a realist, shrugged. 'She told Penny, but Penny knew from other sources anyway. Too many people know the local G.P. You must know that. And if they like him, as they do my father, then they meddle, meaning well, of course. Lots of the older women have severely told Penny she's a lucky girl to have two such worthy men wanting to marry her.

'Off-putting,' Adam commented, with a grin for the absent Penny.

He likes her, Belinda thought. He'd be swayed sometimes too. And in that moment she saw that she must keep that promise, if only to extract a similar promise from Penny. The thought grew and grew. She was a prisoner of a promise made by Penny. Well, why not make it work in reverse, she thought, her excitement growing. To anchor Penny for life to someone who cared, yet who was strong enough to hold her down … but which of those two men? Not the vicar, whose life was such that Penny would never think of sharing it with him. But what about the chemist her father always used? What was his name? George Warren. Not hard up, Belinda considered, and not too old – late thirties. A man who had worshipped Penny, and would probably be quite flattered to have a wife on the stage. But if Penny had hated medicine all her life and in hospital too, would she consent to marry a man whose life was attached to selling medicines? Belinda was so far off in her plotting and planning, that she hadn't realised that Adam was gently squeezing her hand to get her attention.

'My dear, I've spoken to you three times. Where were you?'

'What? What did you say, Adam?' she stammered.

'I remarked that I had just recalled I had never kissed you.'

She met the deep devotion in his eyes and the colour drained from her cheeks. She knew in that moment that if Adam ever kissed her, she would be lost. She felt quite ill at the thought. They would marry and be bedevilled by Penny and have their marriage spoiled. She shook her head, horrified at the thought of such a future.

'Is the thought of being kissed by me so terrifying?' he asked, half amused, half serious.

'Oh, no, no, it's not that,' Belinda said incoherently. 'Adam, I must marry Clive Gregory,' she said. 'No, don't try to dissuade me. Forget all I've just said. I must do it, for a special reason.'

Adam's face went cold with the sudden fear that it might be money that was swaying her; money to settle all the problems. Surely not, not his Belinda! 'Why?' he asked bluntly. 'After what you've been saying to me, why, Bel?'

'I'll keep the promise Penny made in my name, in order to extract one from her. I fully intend to threaten her with telling Daddy and Mummy all about it, and helping Gilbert Orr with his threat that she'd have to come back to hospital no matter what a hash she made of the job. That threat really upset her, and it worked, at the time. I think it will again. She loathes training to be a nurse.'

'Then what will you threaten her with?' Adam asked blankly. He had gone over this question in his mind many times already. Penny was beautiful, charming, exciting and silly, quixotic, slippery as quicksilver, no doubt talented as an actress, but about as prone to keep a promise herself as a fish in the sea. He said so, not quite in those terms, but he got the message over.

'I shall make her promise to marry someone and behave.'

'Not the vicar of your parish, Bel!' Adam said crushingly. 'That would be just plain idiotic.'

'I thought … the chemist?' she suggested.

He thought the matter over. 'You're asking me to agree with you marrying some other chap in order to get your sister settled for life?' He couldn't believe it.

'No, Adam, my dear,' she said softly. 'It's just that I won't risk our life together being spoiled before my eyes by Penny.'

'What life together?' he pointed out harshly.

'Well, what I mean is, I'd rather have a marriage that was no marriage, with Clive Gregory, and keep my dreams of what might have been, than a marriage with you and see Penny tear it to shreds and get everyone's sympathy in the process. You don't know Penny and I do. I've put up with a lot from her, but I couldn't endure that! Not that!'

Belinda went to the shops, alone, with the memory of Adam's set face as he had left her. Hoping even at the last moment to persuade her to change her mind, but being Adam, not resorting to kissing her, in order to sway her. She stuck to her decision, so he left her, another intimate lunch spoiled, and her heart spilling over with grief for happiness that had proved as elusive for her as no doubt it had for Mrs Ivory. Belinda remembered, as she walked unseeingly through the departments of the largest store in Cheppingstock, being set a lesson in school on happiness. 'Write about happiness or draw a picture.' She had elected to draw a picture. She remembered it now. She had little talent for art, but the crude result had been a vivid picture of her mind and her whole outlook. With businesslike speed Belinda, at eleven years, had folded the sheet of paper in half, coloured the top half pale blue for the sky, the bottom half a lurid bright green for the carpeting of the earth. A bare tree bent itself, and a few brown pointed blobs against the sky depicted dying leaves blown before the wind. In that picture was a vivid portrayal of a child's idea of happiness; autumn and freedom and the great outdoors and fine weather and an inner security from cares and anxieties. Her heart ached now, as she thought of it, and wished she could know that kind of happiness now.

She said to the assistant, 'I want an outfit to be married in. An elegant but sober outfit as becomes a quiet wedding to an invalid.' As she said it she heard the last shreds of romance fly away. The assistant looked at Belinda, and judged from her casual yet rather frosty manner that it would not be in order to ask the price range, so she brought three models, the best they had. Dark brown; gun-metal shot with blue; and a black, which Belinda waved away with a shudder. She selected the dark brown. It was trimmed with mink bands. And Belinda, who had never had a fur coat in her life, but who had Mrs Ivory's remark dinning in her ears about being the prisoner of a promise, decided that even a prisoner should have some comfort, so she bought a mink jacket to go with it, and a small mink-trimmed hat.

Adam had said, on that other occasion, that it might be fun to come with her and choose, and carry the dress boxes. Her throat ached as she pushed the tender memory back into the dark recesses of her mind. No pleasure, no thought of what might have been, she scolded herself, and irritably agreed with the saleswoman that mink deserved at least a handbag of crocodile skin, and court shoes to match, and then there had to be expensive underwear, because the practical garments Belinda and her fellow nurses stretched their meagre cash to meet, were an affront to the garment she was to become a wife in. Belinda didn't use make-up, but there was some logic in the saleswoman's discreet suggestion that it might be as well to acquire a good bottle of scent and a much-needed re-styling of her long dark hair, which usually got bundled up into a bun after a session of trying to snatch, unsuccessfully, sleep in broad daylight after night duty. And so it went on. Well, she would be the keeper of the purse strings, so *what*, she thought savagely.

The arrangement was for her to accompany the patient from the hospital to his home. Belinda shrank from her friends seeing her make such a journey. She decided to leave the hospital before, and merely collect him, from home. Home ... what would her father say, she thought, with an anxious little flutter.

Absently she gave her father's address, and had the bill made out to him. She could pay him back later. She found a telephone to call him, tell him what she had done in case the store telephoned him to check on this large bill. But as always, he was out, and nobody knew where he was to be found, as her mother wasn't there. The rest of the day yawned before her, so she telephoned

Gilbert Orr. The scene with Penny might as well be in his flat with him to keep her sister in order, she thought, smiling wryly.

She got through to his flat easily, but wasn't prepared for her reception. 'Bel, love, where have you been?' he roared. 'I've been frantic, searching for you. I waited outside your hospital as long as I dared, but when the press boys appeared, I didn't want to start any more gossip for you by letting them get a sight of me. So I went.'

'Any more gossip? What are you talking about?' she asked blankly.

'Where have you been all day?' he demanded. 'I ask with good reason.'

She fought with herself and decided to be civil and tell him though it hardly concerned him, not all of it, that was. 'First I went to see that girl I told you about – Marcia – and she told me everything. That Steve Rushton had tried to kill her because we'd got her out of his clutches and she knew too much. She apparently hid under a rug in the back of a car of a hit-and-run driver, only she didn't disclose who it was. She escaped from the car to call the ambulance, and then was fool enough to tell Steve about it.'

'Blackmail?' Gilbert grunted, not sounding very surprised.

'Yes, that's it. The family of the driver. Oh, and she was the one who copied my writing and sent the letter to Derek.'

'What on earth for?'

'He was her friend. The only one she could apply to for help to get her free from Brotton Manor.'

'Well, he didn't lift a finger, as I heard it from you!' Gilbert remarked.

'How could he? He thought the note was from me. She meant him to, to be sure he'd come (so she said) but she couldn't get the news through to me to say where she was.'

'A smoky story,' Gilbert grunted. 'I'd believed it if I knew who the people were who were being blackmailed.'

'She wouldn't tell me the name.'

'Now why?' Gilbert snapped.

'Someone was outside her door and she got scared. I think it was Steve Rushton. But she did give me the date of the hit-and-run thing – it was the same date as Clive Gregory got knocked down.'

Gilbert was silent for a few moments, but said at last, 'I wondered when you'd come to that conclusion. Go on.'

'Well, then I went to see Derek, but he wouldn't go and see Marcia.'

'He's gone off her!' Gilbert guessed, disgust in his voice. 'It's you now.'

'Oh, he makes me so angry!' Belinda exploded. 'Anyway, as I left him, Dr Elliott wanted to speak to me, and I had to tell him a lot of things, and we were going up to see

Mrs Ivory, only our conversation got round to Fergus Jopling and the promise. Then Dr Elliott said we'd go and see Clive Gregory, only he was absolutely beastly to me and ordered me to buy things to be married in, in three days' time. Well, he took my breath away. But when he said he was going home that day to see his legal advisers about the Will, Dr Elliott put his foot down and said he wasn't to go out of hospital for another week. That was how it was left. We went out then.'

'So why couldn't I find you?'

'We went up to see Mrs Ivory only Sir Maxwell came out and we heard she was dead. It was awful, poor man. He looked terrible. Oh, it was awful, so ... well, I suppose I looked ghastly, so Dr Elliott took me to lunch. And then...'

'He asked you to marry him, I suppose? You don't think you've kept it a secret who the Big Moment in your life is, do you?'

He sounded so cold and angry. Belinda put her forehead against the cool wall of the telephone booth and said drearily, 'Yes, he did that, Gilbert, and I said yes, I would...'

'So much for the promise!' he interjected bitterly.

'...and then I got to thinking what it would be like in the future and I couldn't bear to see it spoiled. I'm telling you this as a friend, because you've been (and are being) so kind to us about Penny. I decided I'd keep that promise and marry Clive Gregory...'

'Wha-at?' he roared.

'Well, it's what you think I should do, isn't it? Anyway, I thought, why shouldn't I do a bit of promise-extracting. So I worked it out (are you alone, by the way? Oh, good) I thought I'd make Penny promise first to marry one of the two steady people in our village who really want to marry her. If she agrees, then I'll marry Clive. So dear Gilbert, will you let us have this momentous scene in your flat, so you can be umpire, as it were? And give me strength. I shall need it!'

There was no answer from the other end. Belinda thought he must be feeling outraged at such a proposition, so she thought she would add a little request she had just thought of. 'And as my staunch friend, can I ask you (presuming we manage to persuade Penny to make her promise) that you will be standing by me at the wedding, which will take place in the private chapel of Clive's home?'

Then he did speak. He sighed gustily in the telephone. 'I ought to come and fetch you from wherever you're calling from, and tell you face to face, I suppose, but the fact is, I've lived a number of hours this day that I don't want to go through again. I'll tell you on the phone and come and collect you afterwards. Where are you, by the way?'

'Outside Cheppingstock, where we had lunch. I suppose I'm not far from Brotton Manor!' she marvelled. She had forgotten that. 'Can't it wait, whatever it is, till you fetch me, Gilbert?'

'No. I may not have strength to tell you at all by then. The fact is, you expect Penny to be where you left her, with my neighbour Elizabeth. Well, she's not there. She slipped out before Elizabeth was up, and left a note to say she was going home to make a clean breast of everything. Don't blast my ear off, girl! Like you, I don't think she will have turned her footsteps homeward for any purpose. But there it is. Penny is no longer here.'

ELEVEN

Gilbert Orr drove over to collect Belinda in such a short while that Belinda wondered what speed he had scorched at. He looked gaunt, anxious, as well he might. It had been a very bad shock to Belinda, too.

But now he had some news for her. 'The brat has telephoned me,' he said grimly. 'You'll never guess. She's somehow got to London.'

251

'London!' Belinda gasped, her heart sinking. 'What for?'

'She wanted the stage. Didn't I always say she should go on the stage? She's got an audition lined up. I made the mistake of ordering her back on the grounds that she was under-age. I must be getting old myself, to have forgotten that eighteen *is* coming of age, if a girl has a mind to it.'

'Oh, poor Daddy,' Belinda said softly, briefly covering her face with her hands. They were still sitting in the car. Gilbert Orr said, 'Well, never mind about your father. Be sorry for him later. The thing is, I know where she is, and I told her we were coming, and I hinted that her stage career might be considered sympathetically if she didn't fight us. And I thought we might drive to London and still get back in time for you to clock in at the Nurses' Home.'

'Why are you so good to me?' she asked, ill-advisedly.

He looked at her, ardour leaping into his eyes.

'All right, I won't tell you why,' he said shortly, as she fell back before the change in his face. 'You know why. And I'm going to see this thing through. I'm the one to do it. Not this doctor you're in love with. I'm not saying he couldn't, mind. I've looked him over, from a distance. He looks a tough nut to me. Chap after my own heart. But I doubt if he had the advantage I have, in contact with your sister. As the chap who lectures the young nurses, he could hardly shake the breath out of her, as I could, and will, if you don't interfere. Besides, he hasn't taken her out for the evening, as I have!' Gilbert finished grimly.

Belinda felt so helpless that she agreed to go with him to London, and all in all, as they went by the motorway, she felt they could have done worse. It seemed a very short journey.

Penny was staying with two other girls. Belinda didn't recognise them. She watched them go dancing out, calling goodbyes to their date, and she said to Penny, 'I didn't know you had friends in London.'

Penny said sullenly, 'You don't know much about me at all, do you, though you behave as if you know everything!' but Gilbert said shortly, 'Cut that out, Penny!' so she dried up and glowered at them both.

It appeared that the girls were cousins of a friend of Unwin Calder. Belinda saw with dismay that this was Penny's life style. Cadging a roof over her head with some distant connection of a friend's. She looked round the rented room with distaste. It was the untidiest place she had ever seen, crammed to overflowing with the frippery possessions of young women whose sole desire was to go on the stage, and their possessions lay about on the oldest, shabbiest collection of furniture Belinda had ever seen. It was not that the place wasn't clean, so much as that it was botched with the work of many hands. Someone had attempted to splash paint on the bare walls, given up half-way through and tried to cover the bare patches with lurid posters of far-away places, and signed photos of their idols already on the stage. The smell reminded Belinda of the half-stale smell of a theatre that has just emptied, but the thing that appalled her most was that her sister Penny looked more at home here than she had ever done in the Nurses' Home, or even in her own parents' home.

Gilbert Orr said, 'We haven't much time. I have to get Belinda back to the hospital,' but Penny cut in, 'I won't go back!'

Gilbert was equal to this, Belinda saw with surprise. He remarked coolly, 'Did I say you were *wanted* back?' and while Penny took this blow between the eyes, he said, 'We are wondering how you will live, eat, sleep, and buy suitable togs for this new venture, while you're muddling through auditions. You could fail, and then how would you get on?'

'Get a job as a waitress,' Penny said fiercely.

'Very laudable, if you could, the unemployment figures being what they are,' Gilbert said, appearing to give it a lot of thought. 'The thing is, we have an offer to make, but regrettably there isn't much time, so it will have to be a snap decision on your part.'

'I won't give up trying for the stage!' Penny put in quickly. 'I won't go back!'

Gilbert sighed. 'You're just not listening. You are not being asked to give up trying for the stage, though it may be necessary for you to go back temporarily in order to fix all this up, that is, if you're willing to agree.'

'I'm not agreeing to anything you say!' Penny snapped. 'Why doesn't my sister Bel say something?'

'She's had a rotten time these last few weeks, mainly because of you, and as half of this idea is mine, she did agree to let me talk, on the grounds that I'm not likely to waste time breaking it to you gently. You see, I am offering you a chance – a paid chance – to go on the stage. All expenses paid, keep you while you try for that part of your dreams.'

Penny's face lit; excitement, enthusiasm, joy, filled it in quick succession, and then it clouded over with doubt, suspicions and downright loathing of this man who could trick her if she didn't watch out. 'What's the catch?' she asked sullenly.

'You are required to make a promise, just as you forced your sister into making a promise. Well, that's fair, isn't it?'

'I knew there was a catch in it!' Penny observed bitterly.

'Don't you want to hear all about it?' he

asked, half preparing to get up and go, but Penny broke in, 'Let me talk to Bel all by herself.'

'Well, I don't mind, but you'd have to talk to me later, because half of the plan is in my hands to work out, you see,' he explained, and this earned him a surprised glance from Belinda. 'Oh, look, Penny, be quiet while I explain to you,' he urged, with an impatient glance at his watch. 'You've landed Belinda with a marriage she doesn't want.'

'She doesn't have to go through with it!' Penny flared.

'No, that's true,' he allowed. 'Now, without telling your susceptible sister, I have been in touch with the late Fergus Jopling's solicitors. As it happens, I know them. Done business with them before. And I hear that as things stand, this very tricky Will (which I may say you yourself helped to make tricky) stands or falls by the marriage of one Nurse Fenn.'

'Nurse Belinda Fenn!' Penny shouted, suspecting a trap.

'No, love. You messed it all up, being so clever. Nurse Lulie Fenn, you told him, and as "Lulie" doesn't happen to be a given name to your sister any more than to you, it leaves it open, so that either Belinda or you can marry this young man to get the money and do the nursing. Now, if Belinda doesn't want to, then it's you. And you will do it. I shall personally see to that.'

'I don't believe it! Anyway, Daddy won't let me, if I don't want to!' Penny sobbed, getting up and throwing herself into Belinda's arms. Belinda, over her head, raised anxious eyebrows, asking the question: 'Is this true?' of Gilbert Orr, but he merely gave her a devilish grin, and a curt nod. She could take it which way she liked.

'On the other hand,' he said, 'if you promise – before a Notary – to marry someone else, Belinda is prepared to go through with her marriage.'

Penny stopped crying, and looked thoughtfully at Belinda. 'Oh, yes, and you'll be rich, very rich, won't you, Bel?' she said, brightening.

'Well, no, love. And Mr Orr doesn't seem to realise this. The money won't be mine to fling around. I have to be the business head of the companies. I gather I shall be comfortably off, but not rich. And I never said I was prepared to stake you while you messed about in London. But I shall be happy to see you married.'

'Who to?' Penny stormed, feeling tricked again. 'Oh, don't say you've brightly thought up those two tatty suitors Daddy's always talking about – who can see the vicar letting me go on the stage, as his wife? And who can see me marrying stuffy old George Warren, who would want me to serve in his chemist's shop, not go on the stage. Oh, no, it won't do! And I almost believed you!'

'Wait a bit,' Gilbert said imperiously, as Penny snatched up her coat and bag to go storming out into the night. 'There's another chap you might like to consider. One who's quite well off, who would be glad to stake you while you stayed in London and tried to get on the stage, because he likes his own life run the way it is at the moment.'

'Who?' Penny demanded, still suspicious.

'Oh, no!' Belinda whispered, suddenly seeing Gilbert's manoeuvring and not understanding where it was leading, nor liking it a bit.

'Me,' Gilbert grinned at Penny. 'Well, you know I wouldn't want a wife to interfere with my nice life style. I've told you so, often enough. But I'm rich enough for you, aren't I?'

'But you wouldn't marry me when I wanted to, so why now?' Penny demanded.

'I didn't know then that you really wanted something so badly as you want a stage career. I thought you just wanted to be a pest in my life and spend my hard-earned money. Me, I like a girl who's got a star she's hell-bent on following. Now, I'm afraid you'll have to make your mind up quickly, because we have to get back.'

'I can't just make it up in seconds,' Penny stormed. 'What will Daddy say? And

Mummy would never have you as a son-in-law! And you'd have to sign something so you didn't go back on your word about the stage!'

'Gilbert, I want to speak to you, private and personal,' Belinda said grimly.

'All right. We'll go down and see if my car's still in one piece, and then when we come up we'll want Penny's answer: me or the delightful Clive Gregory.'

They walked soberly downstairs until they reached the street and then she turned on him. 'What's in your mind? You never said you wanted to marry my young sister! You're too old! I don't trust you! I–'

'Wait a minute,' Gilbert said, catching Belinda's wrists. 'Think, love. I can't get you, whom I want as I've wanted no other woman. I know where your heart is, never fear. But I can at least smooth your path by taking Penny off your back.'

'But you're not a marrying man. You've said so often enough! And you've also said you pitied the man who got caught with my sister Penny!'

'Yes, and I meant it, but not now. Not now there's a reasonable hold over her. Besides,' he said, delicately, looking away, 'as a matter of fact, I've got my troubles, too, which was the real reason I went up to London to see these legal chaps who aren't my own regular solicitors. Bit of bother with a tiresome wench I've no wish to see again. It was going to be rather a costly business getting rid of her, too. It struck me then, that the best way to avoid this sort of thing in future (my life being the rather complicated thing it is usually) was to take a wife, one preferably who wouldn't be under my feet all the time.'

'Despicable!' Belinda flashed.

'Is it? Or just plain good thinking? With a bit of luck and some useful transferring of cash, I might persuade some chap who's taking a show on tour to put Penny in a good part, and if she went to the States, or even just toured this country ... see what I mean? She'd like that, too. Always on the move, never under the thumb of a demanding husband. Now think, Bel, my love. You'll never be able to hold Penny down unless you let her do what she wants to, and what better than this? And we need not tell her my real reason, need we?'

'You're a very worldly man,' Belinda exploded, with some distaste.

'And you, my love, are the same, though you call it a different name. You say you're a realist, chucking a good man like Elliott, and marrying a pain in the neck like Gregory, just because your sister got you entangled in a promise. Now, admit it, where's the difference?'

Steve Rushton gathered his self-confidence. Things were quiet. Clearly Sir Maxwell was not going to go to the police about him. He had heard no more about Marcia's curious accident. He thought he could form some sort of plan to part Belinda Fenn from some of that money she was to come into. He lay low for a few hours, and slept. Brotton Manor was as good a place as any to hide out, though it was no comfort. At least he was pretty sure that nobody, least of all the owner, would have come there.

And then he got the shock of his life. The newspapers carried a streamer with the news that a young woman with red hair had tried to escape from Spanwell General Hospital because she was afraid someone called Steve Rushton would kill her. She had injured her back and been brought back into the hospital, and although she had not yet said why she feared for her life, a detective was sitting by her side.

The newspaper also carried the story of the nurse who had promised to marry a patient's nephew, and would inherit the vast fortune the patient had withheld from a young man who was crippled and bitter and unable to administer such a vast estate. There was a picture of Belinda Fenn and, beside it ... Steve Rushton.

Steve couldn't believe it. It was his picture, but across the base of it was written, 'To my

Uncle, who expects so much from me.'

Who had perpetrated this joke? And what would be the outcome? His scalp prickled with terror. Someone would soon come forward with the real nephew's photo, and then they would correct the story, and his picture would be before everyone's mind, as the man who had tried to kill a patient in hospital to silence her. What had that stupid Marcia said that for, anyway? He had only threatened her, held her long white throat a second too long in his angry hands. Surely she knew that while he didn't object to a bit of con work, or some mild blackmail for small stakes, he would never stoop to killing? Risky, stupid, that sort of thing. But she was a stupid girl. She must have been, to tell him what she knew, in the first place.

He talked himself into a calm frame of mind, and acted on it. Like Penny, his dreams were of securing a good part on the stage. He had talent, but not quite enough, though he would never admit it. But he knew all about make-up.

He pulled an old wool cap down over his dark hair, and walked into town, to one of the stores, and bought some hair dye. With his crisp dark hair dyed to a rather nondescript brown, and a pair of plain spectacles on, his rounded shoulders and slouching gait replacing his usual straight-backed jaunty walk, nobody would have connected him with the dapper good-looking 'nephew' in the picture. He looked more like a student, in his shapeless sweater and tight jeans. But it was a long walk into Spanwell, and it gave him time to think. He must see Marcia, somehow quieten her and tell her he needed nothing more from her.

He was so busy building speeches and working out how to keep her from crying out (always supposing he got into her room) that he almost missed his opportunity. The Rolls which was taking the lawyers and secretary to Clive Gregory, was pulled up at the side of the road. The unfortunate secretary (doing chauffeur duty in the absence of the regular driver) was under the bonnet, helplessly prodding and pulling at things.

The driver in Steve Rushton's soul boiled over. 'Hey, what are you doing to that engine?' he asked, scandalised.

The secretary straightened up. 'I don't know,' he said nastily. 'Could you do better, and, for instance, make the car go?'

Steve ignored the sarcasm and nodded, pushing the other man out of the way, and when he had corrected the fault, the lawyers hastily agreed that he and not the secretary, should drive them into Spanwell.

That was how Steve Rushton found himself re-engaged for his old job driving the Jopling Rolls, except that he hastily thought up another and quite unexceptional name, so that when Clive Gregory said he wanted to be driven home and was there a decent driver for once, he was told there was a new man called Acton who seemed to understand the car.

There were other changes around Clive Gregory. Sir Maxwell quietly left the hospital and took a holiday he had had owing to him for a long time. Few knew he had made arrangements not to return. His niece and nephew certainly didn't.

Sir Maxwell had never forgiven himself for the job he had done on his sister's eyes, though it could hardly be said to have been his fault. It was one of those things that went wrong, and couldn't, in his case, be forgotten. Perhaps because he and his sister had always been so close. And yet he hadn't been able to trust her case, at the time, to anybody else. He settled up his affairs, took – with some misgivings – an appointment in Africa that had been offered to him some time ago; a chance to study the diseases of the eye at first hand. He hadn't accepted it before, because of Eileen. And now she was gone. But the Spanwell Hospital authorities knew and agreed to release him.

Hope couldn't believe it when she found him packing. He told her he was taking a holiday, alone, and that he had left money in her account to run the household. He had never done such a thing before and there was an air of finality about him, and she wasn't on close enough terms with him to question him. All she could think of was that she now had money to give Oswald, in order to prevent him from involving Lloyd in more trouble with cheques. But it was too late.

She didn't realise that until two weeks later. In those two weeks, Gilbert Orr had married Penny, with the dubious consent of Dr and Mrs Fenn, and Belinda had had her quiet wedding in the private chapel at Clive Gregory's home.

It was known locally as The Abbey. A house built in Victorian times by a newly created peer with a newly amassed fortune, who had no taste and thought it was a good idea to make the house a grim extension of the monastic ruin. The whole place looked like an abbey, was as cold as one, and always chilled the servants into leaving. At the time when Belinda took up the start of her strange new job there was Clive's man, an excellent servant who was somehow devoted to his master, a married couple called Quincey, and the new chauffeur, whose name Acton somehow didn't suit him. He seemed taciturn to the point of rudeness, and always head first in the engine of the Rolls, giving Belinda the impression he not only polished the outside but the engine also.

Clive was more bitter than ever, but a strange excitement filled him, too. In his special chair, he could get about quite well but he was bored. He used to ask Belinda to entertain him, but little by little – as he discovered that she could neither sing nor play a musical instrument, that she didn't like cards or any other game for that matter, and that she had no taste for political discussions he replaced her by his man. The Quinceys, his man and Clive himself would sit far into the evenings playing Bridge or Whist, while Belinda sat within call reading, trying not to think of how strangely things had turned out, and wondering if Gilbert Orr, with his new wife on honeymoon in the Bahamas, was yet regretting his quixotic action to help Belinda. But of Dr Elliott, Belinda rigidly thought nothing. It was still too sore a place in her heart. He, too, had applied to leave the hospital to go back to his old teaching hospital in London. Like Belinda, he found Spanwell too unhappy a place to be in, but unlike Sir Maxwell, he wasn't able to get away.

The excitement began to show in Clive, so that even Belinda wondered what was the matter with him. One day she asked him, and his reply was: 'What would you say if I *walked* in that door soon?' and because she merely stared at him in sheer dismay he told her how he had secretly been contacting the top names in the kind of surgery he would probably require, and that soon he was to be examined to see if and when anything could be done. For Belinda it was the last word in horror, to think of this man, her husband in name, being able to walk. He was a person she could never like. As an active man in the shoes of a husband, Clive would cause her to quake in terror. He would show her no mercy, she was sure.

'When?' she finally managed to ask him.

'Oh, don't worry, my dear wife,' he mocked. 'You'll still be wanted, even if I no longer need a *nurse*,' and even that simple remark he could manage to make hateful.

'I hope the examination will hold out hope of success,' she said formally.

'Well, you will know about it as soon as anyone because you will be there, with me,' he said, his eyes glowing as from a sort of inner fever.

And on the day of his examination, Marcia's life flickered out, like an uncertain light. After all that time of striving to save her, they had finally lost her. Belinda heard one nurse tell another.

Belinda felt choked. She wished there was someone she could talk to about it, but there was nobody. Her one-time best friend, Zoë, had also married because her man had been offered a path lab job in America. Another quick wedding. Nobody took a long time to plan a wedding nowadays, or invite one's friends to throw rice, and leave happy messages around. It was all in a hurry, for a job, or a reason (like Gilbert's to her sister) or her own to Clive Gregory. She couldn't even telephone her father. He only wanted to talk about how soon the time would be when Penny returned from the Bahamas, and to discuss the possibility of her career on the stage. Her mother was interested only in discussing her own health, which had become frail since that last bad bout of 'flu.

Derek, of course, would have gladly talked to Belinda, but Clive knew that he had been Belinda's boy-friend when she had first become a nurse, and there was really no cause to start the flames of his jealousy and bitterness over the Casualty Officer.

So Belinda stood at the window, in that same recess where she and Adam Elliott had stood that day, watching the ambulance and people busy below, and it was almost possible to imagine Adam beside her now.

Sooner than she had expected, Clive's examination was over. His man was helping him to dress and get ready. Sister came to find Belinda, and with her was one of the honoraries, little Mr Pecking, who looked like nothing more important than an anxious vendor of dark and dusty books in one of the small shops down two steps in the town, but who was really very important indeed. He nervously polished his spectacles and said, 'Mrs Gregory? I am so sorry. I have bad news for you,' and he looked as if he were going to cry. Belinda thought, I am the one who should be looking like that! She guessed what was coming. 'Your husband has keyed himself up on a wave of optimism but he should have been told before that there really was no hope.'

Belinda forestalled Sister by saying, in a harsh voice unlike her own, 'I believe he was told, but he refused to believe it. His uncle didn't want him to have hopes, but I have never stood in his way. A person must find out for themselves. He had the right to try for more surgery!'

Sister looked faintly shocked. The honorary put his head on one side in an even more bird-like attitude and shrugged. 'Yes, well, you know best! He is very upset. You will need all your skill … I hear you were a nurse once. You may have a bad time with him. He talks of ending his life rather than stay a permanent cripple. Was he an athletic man?'

Belinda said firmly, because she was too ashamed to have to admit that she knew nothing about Clive's past, before someone knocked him down and rendered part of his body useless. 'He was a man who was quite certain that things should be as he wished.'

'Yes, well, we men are all alike,' the honorary smiled, and with a little chuckle, he patted her hand, hastily became grave, and

269

tendered his commiserations. Then she was alone again.

Now what would happen? She ached to talk it all over with Adam Elliott, but recalling that last time she had seen him, she didn't think he would want to talk to her at all. And he had never even kissed her...

Clive was very awkward about being got into the Rolls. He was unfair to his man, who was so kind and efficient. He was hateful to Belinda, and particularly sharp with the new driver who, Belinda often thought worriedly, reminded her of someone. The way he walked... But he was such a good driver and he did so much love that car. She was glad when they moved off.

Instead of talking to Belinda, however, Clive, seated by her in the back under the fur rugs, kept leaning forward and talking to his driver, and ignoring his man. 'You know I'm not going to be any use, ever?' he asked harshly, and the man said formally, in a soft respectful voice, 'I'm sorry, sir.'

'No, you're not, damn you! You're all right! You've got this car to drive and you love it, don't you? Know what? I think I'll put you on driving my wife's miserable little car and I'll get someone else to drive this. Why should you have any pleasure and not me?'

'As you wish, sir,' the driver said, so Clive whacked his arm with his stick and said, 'Mind your manners! I don't want any cheek from you!'

It was all rather painful. Clive said next, 'What are we crawling for? We're not going to my funeral yet!' and then when the driver pepped up the speed, Clive screamed and shouted that the man would have them all in the ditch. And then Clive commanded that they stop in a lay-by. He wanted to be got out, to sit by the driver.

Belinda was moved to protest. 'Oh, Clive, stay in the back and talk to me,' she begged, but he wouldn't. The driver and his man made heavy weather of moving him, Clive cursing and raving all the time. The disappointment over his surgery had bitten deep into his soul, Belinda thought with compunction.

But at last they were on their way, and Clive settled down to a low-voiced if spasmodic conversation with the driver who, Belinda was surprised to note, hardly answered.

She tried to lean forward to catch what they were saying, but caught the surprised lift of Clive's man's eyebrows, so she sat back in some annoyance. If only the man hadn't been with them! But then things might have been even more difficult.

They seemed to be going the wrong way. Clive was directing the route, getting irritable when the driver didn't speed when he instructed. In fact, Belinda thought, in rising alarm, Clive was giving a good imitation of a back seat driver and even if he were disappointed and annoyed, over the decree of the consultants, there was no need to be so unpleasant to domestic staff on whom he would have to rely in the future. The future, she thought with a shudder; the future, stretching slowly ahead, like a vista of threatening grey skies and bitter cold winds. Why had she done this thing?

Now Clive was looking eagerly out, as if he were searching for someone. With a start, Belinda realised they had doubled back to Spanwell, to the residential suburbs, for here, surely, was the big house that Sir Maxwell and his family occupied, and Clive was trying to make the driver agree to something. 'I am right, am I not?' she suddenly caught Clive say, on a rising note, and moving, she caught the unhappy eyes of the driver in the mirror. She knew him! Her heart started to knock uneasily as she forced herself to put a name to him from the dredging of memory. Steve Rushton! A changed Steve, now with light brown hair and no moustache, and the indefinable change of manner brought by an actor to his new part, changing him subtly from the over-confident, handsome, reckless young man Belinda had last seen him as, into a shy, diffident, but totally dedicated driver of a Rolls that he loved. But Steve Rushton, of all people, as Clive's driver?

She tried to still the thudding of her heart by giving herself a pep talk. What did it matter? Why should she care? Clive needed a driver. She had heard the story of the old one leaving and the secretary making a poor job of combining the duties of chauffeur with the constant cares of taking instruction and dictation from the bad-tempered and demanding Clive. Not everyone's choice of employer. But why should Steve come back into a service he had left?

They crawled slowly past the house of Sir Maxwell and stopped further on. Then Clive, after a muttered conversation with the driver, sat back. Then began a tedious driving round the block, as if he were waiting for something. Had Clive discovered that Lloyd had been the man to run him down? Clive's amusements took curious forms and she already knew that he liked to employ detectives for various odd reasons. One had been at work in the last week. Had this been the reason? For the revenge his uncle had known Clive wanted to wreak out of his own bitterness? But where was the sense of revenge? True, he now had no hope of ever walking, and he was totally unforgiving, but what use would revenge be?

And then at last, what Clive had apparently been waiting for, happened. A car crawled carefully out of the drive of Sir Maxwell's house, waiting to filter into the busy road of traffic. Lloyd Kingston was at the wheel, though it wasn't the car he usually drove, but one much less powerful. He didn't look happy. Hope was beside him, talking urgently. She saw nobody else, recognised nobody. She was just talking urgently to her brother, who was apparently trying to brush off her conversation. He suddenly shot ahead, taking the driver of the Rolls by surprise so that the smaller car, nipping in and out among gaps in the traffic, was soon lost to view, and the more powerful speedy car helpless in pursuit.

Clive shouted: 'Don't lose him! What do you think I've been waiting all this time for?' and he used his stick again on the helpless driver.

Belinda and Clive's man exchanged a glance in which fear was predominant. Her eyes pleaded with the man to do something, but he wanted Clive's wife to speak, so she leaned forward. 'Clive, what do you want them for? Wouldn't it be more civilised to call or telephone?'

He turned round on her. 'Don't be more silly than you can help! I have to catch him when I can! I want compensation from that young whelp – he'll skip the country if I don't catch him now!'

'But that's Lloyd Kingston. He hasn't got a bean to bless himself with,' she said, without thinking.

'And how does my wife know that?' he said, a savage grin splitting his face. 'Doesn't my wife know his mother has just died and left everything to that lout and his sister? And what's wrong with his insurance? Heavens, you've got every penny from my uncle – do you begrudge me the insurance compensation on my accident?'

So that was it. Well, it was no way to go about it, chasing through heavy traffic. 'Why don't you leave it to the detective and lawyers?' she asked reasonably. 'It would be more dignified.' But that was the wrong thing to say to Clive, especially in this mood.

The driver, no doubt thinking to take Clive's mind off quarrelling with his wife and getting into a worse temper, shot forward through a gap and again they were behind the small car, but they hadn't expected it to turn suddenly at the next junction. They lost it again, for there was no space just there for the big car to turn.

In the small car, Hope kept on at her brother. 'Let's close the house. Uncle won't mind. Let's take a holiday, abroad some-where.'

'Run away, for instance?' he shocked her by saying. 'Do you really think I don't know what's going on between you and Vaisey? Do you really think I'm happy about the things he's made me do in the past? Don't you know why? I've been helpless, since that damned hit-and-run accident. Vaisey knew about it. His manipulating of me has been a form of blackmail. And it's got to stop. Know why? I discovered the other day that Uncle Maxwell was being blackmailed for the same thing, by a blighter called Steve Rushton.'

'How – what makes you think that?' Hope gasped.

'That hospital!' Lloyd snarled. 'There we all are, caught in a tight little web. Heavens knows what's going on that we don't know about. Is it like that in every institution where a lot of people work together, seeing the same dreary faces day after day? What was behind that Nurse Fenn marrying that Gregory chap – do you think she'd do it for the money, the way she looked at Elliott? No, there's blackmail of a kind there, too. There must be a way out. There must be!'

'Like Uncle took? Just go away?'

'Uncle Maxwell didn't just go away,' Lloyd said, on a quieter note. 'I distinctly heard him tell Rushton to go jump in the river. He'd get no more cash out of him because the person he had been protecting wasn't there any more – our mother.'

That silenced Hope for a time. She had guessed part of this, but couldn't fill in the details. And now she knew. 'It was Clive Gregory you knocked down?' she whispered.

'Must have been. I didn't know at the time. What I want to know is, how did anyone else know. People like Rushton and your greasy little Oswald.'

Hope winced. She wished her brother hadn't started off hating Oswald quite so much. She wondered drearily why Oswald could claim any finer feelings from herself. She usually railed at him, told him she hated him, but it all came to the same thing in the end. He kissed her protests away and left her ashamed.

'Let's go away,' she said again. 'Away from everything.'

'We will,' Lloyd agreed. 'After we've picked up Vaisey. There's something I want to do today and he's part of it.'

Hope looked at her brother in astonishment. He wasn't going to thrash Oswald, surely? That wasn't Lloyd's style. The easy way out for poor Lloyd, every time! 'Oswald doesn't fight clean,' she warned breathlessly.

'You're telling me!' he retorted. 'Don't worry. No scenes. I'm just going to take him to the solicitors, as I promised I would, and report his blackmailing activities on me.'

Hope was horrified. 'No, Lloyd! Don't be a fool! It will all come out, that you – Lloyd, how did you know you'd knocked someone down?'

'Blood on the front of the car. I was about as drunk as can be, but not so drunk that I didn't feel I'd hit something. Not too drunk to know someone crept out of the back of the car. I suspect it was a girl called Marcia Peters.'

'But that's the girl in the hospital! She screamed out that Steve Rushton had tried to kill her, so they say!' Hope exclaimed. 'Oh, Lloyd, why didn't you drive back that night and see for yourself, and report it. Why?'

'Too drunk to think straight, but not too drunk to think what it might do to mother,' he said curtly, so she was silent.

She was the one who got out when Lloyd stopped outside the block of flats in which Oswald Vaisey lived. Primed by Lloyd, she told Oswald her brother wanted him to go to the bank with him. Oswald laughed. Just threaten a chap like Lloyd enough, especially through his sister, and it would work out all right! He quietly went down with her. They were five minutes all told, but long enough for the Rolls, creeping in at the end of the road, to have picked them up again.

This time Lloyd saw them, and was sure who was in the Rolls. 'Damn, why did I bring this slow monster of yours, Hope! Why does my car always conk out just when I need it?'

Oswald laughed nastily. 'Because you treat it vilely, dear boy! A car needs cosseting, like a woman,' and he kissed the back of Hope's neck.

Lloyd caught the movement, and knew what it was. It sent his temper, uncertain at most times, soaring, so that he shot out from the kerb in front of another car that was just turning out, and earned a blare of Klaxon for his pains. But the car behind formed a screen and the Rolls lost them again.

Now Lloyd had to pull away from them, if he wanted to get to the solicitors. He had caught a glimpse of Clive's face and knew he meant trouble. Lloyd's mind worked over-time. What was Clive Gregory planning? To have his driver thrash Lloyd? Or worse, had he got legal people in his car, to serve a summons or some such thing, to get compensation or retribution? Lloyd wasn't very clear on legal matters, but he had lived under the shadow of what he had done for so long now, that he hourly expected it. But he wanted to do his own punishment of Vaisey first. If he had to be punished, go to prison or whatever might be in store for him, he didn't want to feel he'd left Hope at the mercy of Vaisey, who could apparently per-suade her that he wasn't a bad chap underneath his shady money dealings. Lloyd kept on, and gave the Rolls a run for its money, by using the smaller car to man-oeuvre, and sneak through gaps the Rolls couldn't.

In the bigger car, Belinda had never felt so frightened in her life. The small car's manner of continually pulling away and evading them suggested that Lloyd Kingston was well aware that they were behind him. But Lloyd was used to driving a much more powerful car, which put him at a disadvantage with that one. And Clive was fast losing not only his temper but all sense of reason. He could feel, to his intense irritation, that his driver didn't want to harm the Rolls, and preferred to disregard orders rather than have that precious monster scratched.

'I just want you to pass them and pull in, and make them stop!' Clive yelled. 'Aren't you capable of that?' and another whack from his stick caused the driver to flinch in pain and swerve the big car.

Steve's temper wasn't all that certain either, and as the tension mounted in the Rolls, and Belinda glanced at the hands of Clive's man, gripping the seat beside him, she knew something terrible was going to happen.

'Speak to him, madam! He doesn't know what he's doing!' the man said at last, but Belinda couldn't. She couldn't find words to say to Clive. He never listened to her over the breakfast table, so why should he listen to her now, in the white heat of his excitement and anger? He was crazy with the excitement of the chase. Now they were almost on the small car, held up at the traffic lights. Now they were almost touching its rear. But traffic lights were traffic lights, and had to be observed by the Rolls too. Almost before they had changed, Lloyd had pulled away, and Clive screamed at his driver to catch up, hitting him again in the process.

Belinda found her voice. 'Clive, stop, for heaven's sake! Do you want another accident, so soon?'

Clive turned an angry, working face round to her, snarling, 'Do you think I care? Do you?'

No, she could see he didn't care. She turned dismayed eyes to his man, mutely begging his help. But what could anyone do? Clive had employed others to intercept Lloyd Kingston, and they had failed to make contact. Now Clive was going to do it himself, his way, and nothing would stop him.

The driver evidently decided that he had had enough blows on his left arm, so he put on some speed, and they almost overtook the other car, on this country road that still had quite enough traffic on it to make careless driving a hazard.

Clive didn't want careful overtaking. 'Pull in ahead of them. Make them stop! I want to talk to him!' he yelled.

The driver attempted to explain that it wasn't possible. They could not at the moment get past the other car because they were approaching a bend and there was other traffic coming. But Clive was beyond reason.

Now he had at last caught up with Lloyd Kingston, he had no intention of letting him go.

Lloyd could see him in the driving mirror and was trying to pull ahead, but the car in front of him suddenly slowed down and drew in to the grass verge, the door flying open and a dog being let out. It was something Lloyd hadn't expected. Now he had to swing out, or go into the back of the stationary car, and the Rolls was overtaking him.

Steve knew his beloved Rolls was going to be damaged. He did his best with all his driving skill, to save disaster, but Clive unexpectedly seized the wheel and there was a brief struggle.

Belinda never forgot what happened. It was years before she stopped having nightmares, of a car pulling up to let a dog out, Lloyd hastily pulling out to avoid it, the Rolls already in the act of overtaking Lloyd, and a small van coming towards them. That was always the picture, with Clive struggling to retain possession of the wheel – not the actual crash.

She didn't know it but she was thrown against the door, and the blow to her head knocked her out. She knew nothing of the mêlée of cars and van, nor of Steve's efforts to lighten the impact, nor did Belinda realise that the tangle of locked vehicles began to slip on the far grass verge, going down the slope to a dell, smashing trunks of slender young trees as they went. For Belinda, time ceased to exist for many weeks.

Hope and Clive's man were the only other survivors. They both recovered before Belinda, and from their individual stories, the accident was pierced together. But for Adam Elliott, at Belinda's bedside, it was a living nightmare itself. Would Belinda ever regain consciousness, was the first question. Later, the question was, in what state would she be: this gallant girl who had married a man with no hope of walking again – a young man who counted life as very cheap, and revenge as the most important thing of all. A thing which his uncle had understood and warned her about, but couldn't prevent his warning from sounding melodramatic and therefore useless.

When Belinda did come to, there was a fresh group of nurses on duty, and a different ward sister while the old one was on holiday. By the time Belinda's frame had been removed, and some assessment of her future physical state could be come to, it was high summer. Gilbert Orr, grinning with his own news, had to tell Belinda that Penny had little hope of a stage career just yet; she was expecting a baby, and curiously enough she was thrilled to bits with the idea. So was Gilbert. Where was the man who had been so irritated with Penny's mischief?

Adam, who looked years older, spaced out his news of what had happened in the accident, and to people Belinda knew, so that she connected the news of Oswald Vaisey's death in the accident, with the day that Adam brought in a big florist basket of fine blooms. On a day when he came half hidden behind dark red roses, he reluctantly told her that Steve Rushton had tried to save the Rolls but had been killed instantly, and still most unwillingly answering her searching questions, he told her one day when he brought a picture of Penny cuddling a kitten, of what Hope had disclosed of Lloyd's intentions. Belinda found it hard to believe that Lloyd had at last intended to do the right thing, and it seemed unjust of Fate, to strike him down in that moment.

She found it hard to believe, too, that with Clive's death, she was released from the promise.

'And I don't have to live in that awful dark house?' and Adam had been glad to reassure her on that point.

'And I don't have to have the burden of helping to run those companies and be rich?'

Adam smiled slightly as he shook his head. 'You were scared of that, love, weren't you? No, it all stopped with Clive's death. A lot of the companies will be taken over. Much of

Jopling's money goes to charity. But he did leave you some, for keeping the promise.'

'I'd rather have nothing from him. All I want is my health back. I can't believe I'll ever be active again,' Belinda sighed.

But she was young and strong and determined. She had kept the dreadful promise Penny had made in her name, and in doing so had extracted a promise from her young sister to enter into a marriage on her side which had quite unexpectedly turned out very well. Later, when Penny had, with predictable ease, a jolly little baby, Belinda was painfully walking up and down between supports in the special gymnasium, making her legs work, grimly holding on to the thought of what Adam had said to her, before she took up this pain-filled daily chore.

'My love, I am now asking you to marry me, and there is, so far as I can see, nothing in the wide world to stop us. Not even Hope,' he said quickly, as Belinda's lips stumbled on a question. 'She, quite unexpectedly, decided she couldn't bear to stay in this country any more, and has gone out to join Sir Maxwell in Africa. I don't say she's gone as a nurse or anything useful like that,' he said quickly, as Belinda looked frankly disbelieving. 'But let's hope she meets someone who will help her to take her mind off what's been a far from happy period for her.' He took her hands. 'Bel, love, you do believe me, that I care for you very deeply, very deeply indeed?' which was as far as he could get in disclosing the great depth of his love for her, and the agony he had suffered since she had been brought in from that multiple accident.

'Do you, Adam?' she said, her lovely smile breaking over a face that was losing, day by day, the marks of pain and the world of nightmare she had come through.

'You *do* love me, Bel, don't you?' he asked her anxiously.

She nodded and drew a deep breath to tell him just how much, when Sister popped her head round the door. Bel closed her lips, a resigned smile on her face. Would it always be like this – constantly being interrupted? But just for once, Adam didn't leap up to go. 'I'll be along in a minute, Sister,' he said, and to Bel, he said grimly, 'I am determined to finish this conversation with you – it's the most important of my life!'

But when Sister looked in again later, to see where he was, Adam and Belinda weren't talking at all, but holding hands, looking at each other with such deep happiness in their faces that it hurt to look at. Sister quietly backed out again, and went to find some other doctor for her patient.